TO HELL AND BACK!

*America's First Lady was in the
Oval Office Underneath the Desk While the
Second Lady was out Walking the Dog*

ROBERT E. LEE ELLIOTT

KANGAROO PUBLISHING

Table of Contents

This book is divided into four sections

Introduction

As old as I am standing at the door of death wishing that I could live my life over again. To know and understand the things that I could change and those things that I could never change and the wisdom to know the difference. As you get to be an old person you'll begin to understand life in a different light. Those things in your life that you couldn't understand will become crystal clear to you when the Grim Reaper starts knocking on your door.

You'll find yourself turning to the Lord and asking for a little more time in order for you to get what life you have left in order. Blessed are those that believe in the Lord and follow his teachings for he will prepare a place for them in the Kingdom of Heaven and they will live in paradise forever and ever.

Words that were burned deep in my heart and soul were said by my Lord Jesus as he was dying on the cross. Words that I have cherished my entire life, "Forgive them father for they know not what they do." He will return someday and the day is not even known by the angels in heaven. Oh what a happy day that will be.

At the end of your life you can save your money because you don't need some medical doctor telling you when you're dying because Mother Nature will tell you and it's free of charge. Hard times, rough times and no time is just about what I have left. I don't sugar coat anything I have to say so if you get offended easily then put the book back on the shelf and let someone else read it. The book was not written for the weak of heart or a stupid person because it's common knowledge that stupid can't be fixed.

You can try and reason with a stupid person until you're blue in the face and they'll still be stupid. I have discovered that stupidity and ignorance has no boundaries. Hell will freeze over before a stupid person changes their mind and attitude about anything.

The more I know of the human race the more I love animals. There are only two things that I donate money to, President Trumps campaign and the Asheville Humane Society.

The entire contents of the book is based on the writer's life experiences which you will find hard to believe at times. The authors opinions will be expressed which some people will not agree with but that's their problem not mine. By the time you finish reading the book you'll understand my attitude and the driving forces that can change a person's life without the person even knowing it. I'm just an ordinary old man that's sick and tired of hearing and seeing a completely stupid person shooting their mouth off about something that they know absolutely nothing about. You'll discover how a perfectly innocent person can be railroaded into poverty by money hungry lawyers and mentally afflicted judges.

Dedication

This book is dedicated to myself and all the other people that have been robbed by the myth of Due Process. To the lives that have been destroyed by unscrupulous lawyers making a mockery of the Rule of Law and driving innocent people into poverty and despair.

Foreword

I hereby place everyone on notice that I'm not the usual type of writer that readers expect. I don't abide by standards placed on other writers and what you expect is what you don't get. This book is written in simple and common language for the average reader can understand without the need of a dictionary. There won't be a truck load of fancy words that most people can't understand. Most of all I don't search the internet for subjects to write about.

My writings only reflect my personal experiences and opinions that some people may find offensive. As far as I'm concerned make believe people and stories are just a waste of time and certainly doesn't contribute anything to a person's intelligence. I believe in straight talk and if I feel that a person is an idiot I'll call him one and right now our country seems to be wall to wall idiots.

Before I get into what I think of our system of justice I'll fill you in on my background so you can see where I'm coming from and how I got here. Rest assured I didn't ride into town on the back of a cabbage truck and I refuse to join the ranks of a fool.

I'm a retired police officer having served twenty five years with the Dade County Sheriffs Office in Miami, Florida. I served eight years with the United States Naval Reserve with the last two years in the Construction Battalion better known as the Sea Bees. I hold an

Associate of Arts Degree from the Miami Dade Community College, a Bachelor of Science Degree in Criminal Justice from Florida International University and a Master of Science Degree in Public Administration from Biscayne College also located in Miami, Florida. I will compare my educational credentials with most people and especially other authors.

When writing I don't waste my time with make believe people and stories. Fiction is basically a waste of time and when you get as old as me time is of the essence. I'm just a crippled old man that just turned eighty five years of age and no doubt living his last years on God's green earth. It seems like my life's journey has been one mountain after the other until I'm tired of climbing. I'm always reminded of that song by singer Eddy Arnold when he sang "Make the world go away and take it off my shoulders because this time Lord you've given me a mountain that I may never be able to climb."

I've been robbed and destroyed by what they call Due Process which will be explained in the story of the book. Just bear in mind that what you read has actually happened as hard as it is to believe. My experience with miracles that re-enforced my belief that Almighty God is with me in everything I do.

Read about how the writer's trip to hell cleared his mind as well as his vision in dealing with people. A road paved with lying ass lawyers and a couple brain dead judges that couldn't careless about justice and a citizens constitutional rights. Like I've said before ignorance knows no boundaries and that also includes judges and lawyers. I've testified before hundreds of judges during my twenty five years in law enforcement and some couldn't hit their ass with a bow fiddle. I had to arrest one that tried to bribe me and he got five years in the state prison. That was during the time that most people had respect for the law. If it happened today the lawyer would probably get at least ten days and it would be served on probation if he got that. For myself I wouldn't trust a lawyer any further than I could throw his or her ass. Don't believe any of that bullshit regarding privileged communication between a lawyer and his client. If you actually believe that your conversation with your lawyer is protect- ed then you have no idea what's going on. All the lawyers belong to the same organizations and drink at the same watering holes and spend most of their time telling other lawyers about their clients. Code of Silence, what a joke.

The Story

I was born poor as hell in a dirt poor little town in Northern Alabama. All my brothers and sisters were born in the same old bed in the same old broken down farm house. The only light bulb that I ever saw burning was hanging in he middle of the intersection of the main highway and the main street of our little town. Don't be misled by thinking our main street was something to behold because it was nothing but a dirt and gravel road. It could best be described like the main streets in the Western movies of long ago. Our main street only had wooden sidewalks on one side of the street. At the end of main street there was an endless supply of spring water running out of a pipe coming out of the ground that everyone got a drink from and the water is still running to this day.

Our house didn't have electricity, running water or indoor plumbing. There was no such thing as having a bathroom or toilet in your house. Our toilet so to speak was an outhouse located 15 or 20 yards in back of the house. If anyone had to go after dark they'd use the slop jar usually located underneath their bed. My mother never knew what it was to have an electric stove or refrigerator until we moved to Miami, Florida in 1942. In Alabama all family members were introduced to hard work at an early age and knew what it was to work all day in a corn or cotton field in 90 degree heat.

TO HELL AND BACK!

Our school house had only one large room that was divided up into sections for grades one through sixth with only one teacher. The students in higher grades were taught on different days. There was no such thing as a cafeteria and if you didn't bring something from home for lunch you didn't eat. My lunch container was an empty lard bucket and I could always depend on my mom packing me a peanut butter and jelly sandwich with a piece of home made pie and a peach.

When it was harvest time school was always dismissed at noon so the students could go home and help their parents work in the fields. Now days you can't get a kid to mow the lawn much less have them hoe corn and pick cotton all day long. I have followed my mother picking cotton as a very young boy and watched her fingers bleed from the sharp cotton pods. I've seen my father so tired and exhausted after working all day he would lay down on the porch and fall asleep.

The family lived from hand to mouth and even as a young kid I knew that life had to be better than how we were living. It was ironic when someone would get mad and tell you to go to hell because you were already there. I never heard the term poor and actually didn't even know what it meant. I often wondered why people would leave a basket of food at our front door. Now that I look back on my life it was before the food stamp program was created because other good people could see that we didn't have anything to eat by the way we dressed I suppose. There's no doubt in my mind that God will reward those caring and loving people.

Whenever a storm would come up my mother would take all of us to the storm shelter that my father made for us. It was a cave that he dug into a large bank next to the highway in front of our house. Mom would take a kerosene lamp and some blankets because we always had to stay all night long. I believe that mother kept us there all night because she was always scared that the house might fall down from a real high wind. I remember laying there on a bench listening to the wind blow and hearing the door rattle until I fell asleep.

The next morning mother would slowly open the door and be so happy that our house was still standing. Sometimes I thought that we would be better off moving into the chicken house because it looked better and stronger than our house. How any family as poor as we were and survived still amazes me to this day. If it wasn't for rabbits, squirrels and polk salad I know we would have starved to death.

Every time I hear Dolly Parton sing that song about the coat of many colors that her mother made for her I knew that she must have lived a poor country life like I did. My mother made my clothes out of empty flour sacks and I was glad to get them because I knew that I'd never get any store bought clothes. For the length of my young life I wore the clothes handed down to me from my older brothers. The kids these days don't appreciate what they have because they've never been without. Today they have play grounds with swings, slides, basketball courts, ping pong tables and the list just goes on and on. My play ground back in Alabama was a back yard next to a lumber yard, a train track and a large saw dust pile created by a lumber company.

My mother worked the fields of close by farmers for a wage of next to nothing in order to buy flour, lard and whatever else she needed for cooking. Needless to say we ate a lot of biscuits and gravy. My father started working for the Frisco Railroad Company making two dollars a day which didn't go far with a wife and seven children at home. The family simply couldn't make it on such a small income and dad decided to go to Miami, Florida and look for work. He found a job at the Tropical Awning and Shutter Company for a couple years. He was still working there when mother arrived there with the entire family. Finding a place to stay on such short notice was a trick to behold but we'll go into that later.

TO HELL AND BACK!

My mother had to leave Alabama because there was nothing else to do. It was just too much on her to even try and attempt alone so she decided to sell the entire place for one thousand dollars which included eighty acres, our house, a chicken house, a corn crib and a store on the highway. She made the decision to move to Florida so we could be with our father too because it was apparent that we'd never survive on our pathetic little farm in Alabama. Mother hired a coal truck driver by the name of Muntz eighty dollars to move us to Miami, Florida. We put everything we owned in the back of the truck including ourselves and covered it with a large tarp. Thank God our mother got to ride in the cab of the truck. Rest assured it was no fun riding in the bed of a coal truck covered with coal dust. No doubt we must have been a sight to see by other people because it surely reminded them of the Beverly Hill Billies moving to California.

In Alabama we lived a primitive life style always having to scratch for a living. There was no hope for the future and that was why we all were in the back of a coal truck heading for Florida. It was an act of desperation in seeking a better life. Going into the unknown can be scary but when you have nothing to lose it doesn't matter if it's scary or not.

There's a million stories to be told but I'll never live long enough to tell them because I'm an eighty five year old cripple in poor health living the twilight years of my life. It seems like a person gets smart too late in life. Let me tell you of something that happened in my life that re-enforced my strong belief in God. I don't tell make believe stories and this incident is the absolute truth so help me God. One night my wife had a nightmare and woke me up screaming wildly in bed. I woke her up and the first words she said was "Bobby, thank God it was only a dream." She said that a man knocked on our front door and handed her a note which said "Lydia is going to die." Lydia was her sixteen year old sister who wasn't even sick at the time.

Within three days her father called our house and told my wife that he had to take her sister to the hospital because she had gotten sick. My wife jumped into our car and raced off to the hospital without me. I had to call my brother to take me to the hospital and I told him about the dream that my wife had a couple days earlier and hoped that she wouldn't remember having it. Within two days her sister died and I will never forget that day of September 6, 1959 as long as I live. A day that God gave evidence of his ever lasting presence among us.

Between Lydia's death and the broken door at our new house, let no man tell me that there's no God. I know him, I've met him and I will never deny him. One time when I was a young teenager my older brother and I were rough housing in our new house when I fell against a bedroom door and completely broke the entire face of it. It was broke beyond repair and I was scared out of my wits for my father and mother to see it. A beautiful cedar door and I knew that my parents would be extremely angry and never forgive me. I was scared and disappointed in myself and got on my knees and asked the Lord to help me. I had never prayed so long and so hard for anything in my young life. Crying and begging Jesus to please help me.

What I tell you is the gospel truth and you can believe it or not but when I stood up and opened my eyes the door was like new without one bit of damage to it at all. Don't tell me that God doesn't answer or work miracles because I know better. One thing for certain everything you own on earth is only yours temporarily, I'm in the process of getting rid of all the things that I collected and held dearly because as soon as I die someone else will own them.

As I continued my journey into manhood my faith was tested many times. It seemed like I had one mountain after another to climb. Some things you never forget and carry it to your grave. For example my first wife told me that "I made her skin crawl." A sad thing to say to a man that tried to be a good father and husband. A man that was so broke he never carried anymore money in his pocket than twenty five cents. A man that never stopped for lunch because he never had enough money to buy himself lunch. After all of that it was a crushing blow to hear your wife tell you that you made her skin crawl.

After trying to get over my divorce I was told by a woman I was dating that "If I can't have you no one will" which was an obvious threat on my life. It got to the point that I simply couldn't understand how women think and quite frankly I still don't. One thing for sure there are some people that should never get married. A man thinks that his new wife will stay the same and the woman thinks she can change her new husband. Both are wrong but they find that out after it's too late.

The older I get and know people the more I love animals and dislike humans. One species of humans you need to stay away from is lawyers unless you don't care about losing all your money. Lawyers are trained on how to screw people out of their money and if you believe they represent truth and justice then you must have your head up your ass.

My life was destroyed by lying ass lawyers and two brain dead judges that made a mockery out of truth and justice. If you're interested in finding out how easily you can lose your ass by Due Process then read the book "Kangaroo Justice and Well Dressed Thieves With a License to Steal." The book will give you a brief summary on how it's done. A story beyond belief on how you can be robbed of your life and there's nothing you can do about it.

In 1998 I had a trailer trash couple produce and distribute hundreds of slanderous posters with my wife's picture all over the county and even on the front door of our church house where my wife sings in the choir. They posted them on all the power poles in the neighborhood and put them in all our neighbor's mail boxes. Then they distributed them in shopping centers and passed them out to pedestrians at busy intersections. They have been trashy freeloaders their entire married life ripping off every welfare system they could get on.

The husband claims to have a disability and has defrauded the Florida disabilities act for years among other welfare systems. He has all the traits of a sexual predator and hangs out at work out gyms where he can easily find half naked women in need of additional sex. His wife is a dedicated psychopath in need of medical help and should be in a mental hospital. To hide their life style they attend a Baptist church in Plantation, Florida presenting themselves as Christians. In short ACJ and DEJ are the two biggest hypocritical and assholes walking on God's green earth. The wife spends most of her time following her husband around all over town to see who he's trying to screw instead of her. You've never known real trailer trash until you meet these bums.

Now here comes the strange part. I sued the trash for slander and libel and won a thirty five thousand dollar judgment against them. They hired a lying ass female lawyer in Fort Lauderdale, Florida that we will refer to as Douche Bag Mary of the Grunt and Dump law firm. She filed bankruptcy for the trash because they owed thirty two other creditors beside my judgment. I never tried to collect on my judgment because they were just common trash with nothing and are still trash to this day.

My judgment was about to expire due to the ten year limit and I decided to have it renewed considering what they had done to my wife and I. I hired a lawyer in Asheville to renew the judgment and he didn't even bother to check to see if the judgment was still active. Within a week he was informed by the trash that my judgment had been satisfied by a bankruptcy court in 2003 which my wife and I knew nothing about. We were never notified by the trash or their sorry ass lawyer. I contacted their lawyer Douche Bag Mary on several occasions asking her why she didn't notify us of the satisfaction of the judgment and she told me that it was my problem not hers and hung the phone up in my face.

The next thing I know the silly bitch filed an affidavit against me stating that "I knowingly and willfully violated a court order" and the court issued a summary judgment against me.

To make a long story short the court awarded the trash a $171,000.00 judgment against me and a superior court judge in Asheville, North Carolina signed an order that gave me twelve days to pay the trash $125,000.00 or he'd have the sheriff auction off our house and all of our personal property including everything we owned.

Needless to say it pissed me off royally and I wrote letters of objection to the superior court judge and the lawyer that represented the trailer trash in court. I also wrote letters to both North Carolina state senators and the state's Attorney General in an effort to obtain information regarding the state law of "Tenants in Common" and "Tenants by the Entirety" and never received a response from any of them. I even wrote to the North Carolina Supreme Court for an opinion and was also ignored. Apparently a complaint from an ordinary citizen doesn't carry much weight with the court or anyone else in the legal system.

The superior court judge in Asheville and the lawyer representing the trailer trash finally got tired of my letters and answered me. I will reproduce the letters that I sent to them so you can better understand my frustration being a victim of the so called justice system and how easily you can be robbed of everything you have and no one other than yourself gives a damn.

The first letter to the superior court judge is simply asking him why?

September 17, 2019

Hello Judge,

I hope this note finds you and your family doing well and in good health. Please forgive me for bothering you but ever since I had a hearing in your courtroom back in 2016 I'd still like to find out how or to understand how I got robbed.

The lawyer arguing the case against me had absolutely no proof that we had ever gotten a divorce. He couldn't produce one document or one iota of proof that we had ever gotten a divorce because it never happened.

You had laying before you a picture of the slanderous poster of my wife and a very complete explanation of what had transpired between me and the trailer trash that was suing me. Quite honestly I didn't even feel that you even recognized that my wife and I were in the courtroom because during the entire hearing you didn't even ask me one question even though you had a world of information lying in front of you.

Just to refresh your memory about the particulars of my case I'll start with the lying female lawyer in Fort Lauderdale, Florida who had been suing me since 1998. I had obtained a judgment against her free loading clients for producing and distributing hundreds of slanderous posters with my wife's picture all over the county. They even posted them on the front door of our church house where my wife sings in the choir. They posted the slanderous posters on all the power poles in the area of our house, to all our neighbors and even in the windows of nearby stores and in the Asheville shopping center. They would actually stand on the corner near our neighborhood and give them to passing motorist and pedestrians.

I never tried to collect my judgment because I knew that they were just poor trash that had nothing and milking the welfare systems in every way possible. I can't name them because I was forced to sign an agreement that I would never mention their names and I certainly don't want to violate the agreement.

When the summary judgment was filed against me it was based completely on a lie that the Fort Lauderdale lawyer admitted to me on two different occasions. My wife and I had renewed our wedding vowels in the Buncombe County court house four years before the summary judgment was ever issued. We have been married for going on forty years.

My wife and I were never notified that my judgment against the trash had been satisfied in 2003 by a bankruptcy court. When I renewed the judgment the lawyer that I hired to do it failed to even verify if the judgment was still in effect. I called the lawyer in Fort Lauderdale on numerous occasions asking her why we weren't notified of the judgment satisfaction and her response was "that's your problem not mine and by state law I don't have to notify you of anything."

Then of all things she files a lawsuit seeking a summary judgment because I "knowingly and willfully violated a court order" which is a barefaced lie and she knows it.

I wrote the judge scheduled to hear the case and informed him that the lawsuit was based completely on perjury but he seemed to careless. The court date was set and I requested a continuance to give me enough time to borrow the money for the trip and to find someone to take care of my mentally disabled son in my absence. The judge refused my request which I couldn't understand for the sake of me and held court without me.

During the hearing in your court you accepted the lawyer's argument about my wife and I being divorced even though no proof was presented. Your decision was based on "information and belief" which goes against the very concept of justice where a person is "innocent until proven guilty." It appears that hearsay and a person's biased opinion completely over rides proof.

If this is your idea of justice I want no part of it. When you accepted the lawyers allegation of the divorce you ruled that we were "tenants in common" denying us the protection of "tenants by the entirety" and opened the door for every money changer in town to take our property.

Maybe it doesn't mean anything to you but it does to my wife and I. Your decision was wrong then, wrong today and it will still be wrong tomorrow. It effectively destroyed what life I have left.

I served twenty five years on the Sheriff's Office in Miami, Florida and I've never witnessed such a miscarriage of justice.

Yours truly,

Robert L. Elliott

The following is the second letter that I wrote to the superior court judge questioning his ruling regarding my case.

September 29, 2019

Hello Judge,

I wrote you a note almost two weeks ago asking you a simple question and still haven't received a response from you. I would really appreciate you giving me an explanation on how your ruling against me was justified by law. The lawyer Mr. Mays, tells me that he didn't need any actual proof that my wife and I had ever gotten a divorce and all he needed was "information and belief" that a divorce had occurred according to state law.

The question of a divorce came up because of a decision I made when it became apparent to me that my lawyer was having more conversations with Mr. Mays then he was having with me disregarding "privileged communications between a lawyer and a client." I got the opinion that the "Code of Silence" was nothing more then a myth. I pushed the false narrative to my lawyer that I was going to get a divorce because I knew that he would tell Mr. Mays and I was in the false belief that I thought if all the lawyers believed I was divorced and didn't have anything they'd get off my ass. They bought the story of a divorce hook, line and sinker but that didn't stop them for a minute in their insatiable appetite for money. Mr. Mays couldn't produce one document supporting his argument or one iota of proof because it never happened.

Now maybe everyone can understand why something like "information and belief" should never over ride proof. I can't seem to find any where in the state laws where it pertains to the so called "information and belief" where it is accepted over proof. Maybe you'll be kind enough to let me know where and if it exist.

Even if there is such a ridiculous amendment to a statute it was definitely wrong in my particular case because what Mr. Mays was trying to prove in vain didn't actually exist. Under no circumstances should hearsay and one man's biased opinion over ride proof.

When you have nothing to do and plenty of time to do it in please weigh what you and the lawyers have done to my life. I'm disappointed that you didn't look at and read my full explanation of what had occurred during the twenty years that I had been harassed by the Florida lawyer who obtained a summary judgment against me under perjury admitted to me on two different occasions.

You never even recognized my wife and I were even in your court room or ask one question of me. The only thing I heard you say during the entire process was you saying "draw up the order and I'll sign it." Is that all it meant to you?

Between you, Mr. Mays and the lawyer Mary Cuntwell in Florida, I think all of you bastardized the concept of The Rule of Law. I served twenty five years in law enforcement and thought that I had seen it all until I sat in your court room that day.

I hope you're a happy man and live a long happy life because it appears that you have done quite well on a judge's salary.

Yours truly,

Robert L. Elliott

TO HELL AND BACK!

The last note that I sent to the judge finally got a response for me. The subject of the note was the state law pertaining to "tenants in common" and "tenants by the entirety."

OCTOBER 1, 2019

Good morning sir,

I hope this note finds you well and doing fine. If you have a few minutes I'd really appreciate you explaining the state law pertaining to "tenants in common" and "tenants by the entirety." I'd like to know where in a state law that it accepts "information and belief" over proof.

Proof and nothing else must be the only thing acceptable to avoid mistakes like your court made in my particular case causing great harm to a person's life.

For a court to accept hearsay and a man's biased opinion over proof is a complete miscarriage of justice. I was wronged by you, Mr. Mays, the lying Florida lawyer who wears perjury on her sleeve as a badge of honor and even my own lawyer who didn't understand or accept the concept of "privileged communication between a lawyer and his client."

I realize that I'm just a nobody as far as you are probably concerned but rest assured my life is just as important to me as your life is to you. I don't have any money because you and the lawyers robbed me of what I had but I still want to know how you twisted the law to do it.

It seems like anyone wearing a suit and carrying a briefcase are better at robbing people then John Dillinger or Jesse James and they don't need a gun and a mask.

Please send me the information that I requested and if you want to be a good guy tell all of those who stole my money to return it to me. Awaiting your reply I remain.

Yours truly,

Robert L. Elliott

The last letter finally got me a response from the judge and he didn't have much to say. He never answered my question and told me that if I thought his ruling was in error to go hire a lawyer. Go hire a lawyer? Apparently he doesn't understand anything I've said. Eventually someday there will be pay back for what the sorry bastards have done to me.

A tid bit of information for you. Did you know that 51% of all the people in congress are millionaires? Corruption my dear citizens corruption. Something else that will help wake you up. Recently the authorities discovered almost twenty three hundred unborn little babies in a doctor's basement preserved in mason jars. Terrible isn't it but it's not a drop in the bucket compared to the murders conducted by Planned Parenthood. Since 1973 so called abortion which is nothing but legalized murder killed 60 million unborn babies. The world condemns the Socialist Adolph Hitler for killing 6 million adults and there's no comparison.

Someday the blacks will wake up and realize that Planned Parenthood is destroying their race. Thank heavens we have a good man like Kanye West standing up for Jesus and telling his people to support President Trump. Anyone that attends one of his services appreciates him and has nothing but praise for him.

The only way the gun problem can be resolved or at least suppressed is to enact my suggestion but bear in mind it will never be completely eradicated because criminals will always be able to get guns. Anyone trying to buy a firearm has to be at least twenty one years of age and has to prove with documents that they have no criminal record or a history of mental illness. It shouldn't be the government's responsibility to check on a person's state of mind and past.

The second amendment to the Constitution was created and placed in the Constitution because our country didn't have a militia to speak of and it was up to the citizens to protect and defend our country from foreign and or domestic aggressors. Our forefathers were more concerned about the defense of our country than duck hunters and the likes. Hunters and gun nuts have always thought that the second amendment was created just for them.

Do you ever think about writing a book? Well save yourself a lot of heart ache, aggravation and money, forget the idea. Getting the book published is one thing but trying to market your book will be an exercise in futility because you're an unknown author. Have you noticed how almost everyone on Fox News and appears on Fox News has written a book which they advertise on the station to millions of viewers. A book can be advertised on Fox News by the author and within two days if not immediately become The New York Times best seller and be shown on the Barnes and Nobles website and placed in book stores.

An unknown author will play hell trying to market his book because the system seems to be stacked against him. Unless you're well known you don't have a chance. A well known author could write about a hemorrhoid and within a day or two it would be listed as The New York Times best seller and be all over the internet and in book stores. It seems like everyone writes about the political situation that exist today involving President Trump and if you want to be completely confused try reading them. Everyone has an opinion and you know what they say about opinions, they're like assholes everyone has one.

If you'd like to see how some authors saturate the internet with their books go to the Amazon and Barnes and Nobles websites and you'll see the same authors over and over. They can fart and make it a best seller within a week.

Almost all of the books are fiction of make believe stories and people which is nothing but a waste of time as far as I'm concerned. I only write about my life's experiences and what I know is true. I don't abide by the rules and have yet to find another author that compares to my style of writing. Being an author will cost you your ass financially because getting a book published and on the market will cost you in the neighborhood of $3,500.00. There's no guarantee that you'll get back ten cents in royalties so beware of the financial risk that you're taking.

I operated under the belief that the title of a book should be so provocative that it would attract attention of readers and get it on the internet which seemed reasonable to me. That belief must be flawed in some respect because I've written five books and have yet to see any of them on the websites of Amazon or Barnes and Nobles. Well, enough of my book problems for awhile.

When I was a young boy my father would ask me "If I thought I was ever going to amount to anything?" Well, I didn't know then and I still don't know. Being successful certainly doesn't bring happiness otherwise so many successful people wouldn't be getting divorced. Of course there's a lot of people that should never be married in the first place because they're not suited for it. Just like there's a whole lot of young people that should never attend college.

I've said it before and I'll keep saying it until hell freezes over. There are certain people that should not be entitled to a trial. If an individual is apprehended in the act of murdering someone and there is absolutely no doubt of his guilt then it serves no purpose to waste the tax payers money on having a trial. Either hang the sorry bastard in the public square and let him rot there or feed him alive feet first into a wood chipper so he can see himself being fed into a hog pen. Mark it down and put it in the bank because Plato's prediction of long ago will come true for sure regarding our country.

Sometimes I think that I'd be better off being back on that run down little farm in Alabama. Working in a cotton or corn field making starvation wages then being on a police department in a large crime ridden city. At least while working in a field you didn't have to worry about being shot.

The life in the big run down cities like Chicago, Detroit and Baltimore are good examples of how the mayors and local governments can utterly destroy the quality of life. Look at Los Angles and San Francisco California and witness the decay and largest open septic tanks in America. Thousands of homeless people and bums sleeping in tents and boxes along the main highways into town. The sidewalks and street serves as their toilet. They live on top of each other and the sidewalks are covered with feces, urine, needles and used condoms.

The state of California has been declared a sanctuary state by the lame brain governor. The people of California deserve the idiots that they have elected to run the state and the sooner the state drops off into the Pacific ocean the better off America will be.

All of us were born ignorant but some people work hard as hell to be stupid. It's like actor John Wayne said "Life is tough but it's a lot tougher when you're stupid." It's like I said on the cover of one of my books "It's impossible to fix stupid."

Regarding myself I was driven to destruction by lawyers, judges and a court system that found me guilty without even considering that I could be innocent. I soon discovered that the concept of Due Process and the Rule of Law was a myth. I was sued by the same lying ass female lawyer from 1998 to 2016. I could fart and she'd try and make a federal case out of it. She was tagged and known as Douche Bag Mary because she looked so much like a douche bag. She works in a law firm with her naive husband and another relative who appears to be short on brains like her husband. If you ever need a crooked lawyer just call the Grunt and Dump law firm on West Broward Blvd in Fort Lauderdale, Florida. Rest assured they're good liars and will say and do anything to win the case for you.

Hopefully, someday I'll locate someone that can explain "information and belief" to me and tell me where I can find it in the North Carolina statutes. I even wrote to Josh Stein, the North Carolina Attorney General and his office wouldn't or couldn't tell me either. I've written to both North Carolina state senators, a judge and even the North Carolina Supreme Court and still can't get any explanation on how "information and belief" can over ride proof as was testified to in a court of law. Apparently the court that I appeared in considered me guilty until I could prove that I was innocent. No documented proof of my guilt was ever produced to the court stating that my wife and I had ever been divorced yet the presiding judge ruled that we had been divorced at some unknown time which was a lie. The judge ruled that having proof of a divorce was not necessary and he stuck with his idiotic ruling violating the very basic concept of justice where a person is innocent until proven guilty of anything. The judge was wrong then, he's still wrong today and he'll still be wrong tomorrow. In his ruling he made a mockery out of justice and apparently has been on the bench far too long. I've written numerous letters to the judge asking him to explain his ruling to me and how he was able to disregard proof so easily? I served in law enforcement for twenty five years and never heard of anything like "information and belief" being considered as proof.

After numerous letters to the lawyer representing the trailer trash I finally received a response from him explaining his position in the matter. He stated that he had received an order from a bankruptcy court to the effect that the judgment against me was the result of "willful and malicious" conduct on my part and therefore not dischargeable in bankruptcy. Maybe I've lost my cotton picking mind because that is nothing but bullshit. The only malicious people involved in my case were the trailer trash who produced and distributed hundreds of slanderous posters with my wife's picture and the sorry lying bitch of a lawyer in Fort Lauderdale, Florida that represented the trash that was suing me. That sorry bitch wears perjury on her sleeve as a badge of honor.

In the lawyer's letter of response he stated that he drew the conclusion by himself that my wife and I had divorced and remarried which made us "tenants in common" by state law even though he couldn't prove diddly squat. I'm convinced that the presiding judge hearing the case didn't know his ass from a hole in the ground regarding the law and I still want to see it for myself. The lawyer stated that he felt that he did a good job and it was fair that I only had to pay the trailer trash $125,000.00 instead of the full amount of the judgment. Isn't that nice of him I only had to pay them $125,000.00 for producing and distributing hundreds of slanderous posters of my wife all over the county and even on the front door of our church house. Even with this knowledge the court ruled that I was "willfully malicious" and the trash were perfectly innocent of any wrong doing.

Needless to say this is a good example of why I have absolutely no respect for lawyers and judges because both specialize in throwing people underneath the bus and have a warped perception of justice.

Always bear in mind what Plato predicted many, many years ago when he said that the condition of society will get so bad that even the puppy dogs will raise up on their hind legs and demand their rights. The people will vote for anyone that will restore order. Our country is fast approaching that point and the only person capable of stopping it is President Donald Trump.

Anyone with half a brain will thank God every day for President Trump and as far as I'm concerned his image should be engraved on Mount Rushmore. He's a true patriot and a fighter for America and the best thing going for him is the fact that he's not a lawyer.

Are you aware that 84% of the people in congress are lawyers? No big wonder that 51% of them have become millionaires and most are multi-millionaires. It's such an easy way of becoming rich by just sitting on your ass and doing nothing as you count the ways of ripping off the tax payers. It only requires part time work and the assholes should only be paid part time wages. No wonder they are against term limits and be forced off such a gravy train.

At present the Democratic Party is in complete disarray and are trying to get crooked Hillary to run again because all of the present candidates are flaming assholes that don't have a chance of beating President Trump in the 20/20 election. Just look at the candidates. They have a wild haired Socialist with a heart attack, a Socialist minded woman that passed herself off as an American Indian in order to obtain preferential treatment and lied about why she left the teaching profession. Behind them they have a crook and a cocksucker that no doubt has his brains in his pants.

I always try and be opened minded when listening to other people's point of view but never so open minded that my brains fall out onto the floor. I listened to President Trump's speech at the rally he had in Minnesota and I totally agree with him when he said that the only thing sleepy Joe Biden was good at was kissing Obama's ass.

Have you noticed how Obama doesn't want to have anything to do with Biden running for president? He doesn't want any attention being brought to him because he knows that his knowledge of the conspiracy to over turn the 2016 presidential election will eventually come out. As big and widespread as the conspiracy was and still exist it would take an idiot to actually believe that Obama wasn't aware of it. The Attorney General William Barr just recently stated on national television that there has been an active effort to undermine President Trump's administration ever since he took office.

Almost every large city controlled and run by liberal Democrats is in ruins and chaos. If you've read the previous letters that I've re-produced and written about you'll understand why I'm such a strong believer that being a lawyer should disqualify a person from hold-ing public office. I was in law enforcement for twenty five years and most of the lawyers that I had to deal with couldn't hit their ass with a bow fiddle. They always thought that they were something special and smarter than everyone else. Apparently all of them majored in a required course of How to Steal 101. Learning how to twist the law and lying under oath is an accepted practice and admired by other lawyers in their profession.

The more I think of how I was accused of being "willfully malicious" by a lying ass lawyer the more it pisses me off. I suspect that the judge in Fort Lauderdale, Florida that accepted such a sworn affidavit from the female lawyer was getting more from her then money. Having an orgasm on top of a desk certainly doesn't justify what the sorry bastards have done to me and someday they're going to have to stand good for what they've done to me.

Between the trailer trash, lying ass lawyers and a couple of brain dead judges I totally give up on the so called concept of Due Process. If what I've been through is called justice then everyone in the legal system can stick their idea of justice up their ass for all I care. Lawyers are nothing but well dressed thieves with a license to steal . They can rob more people with a briefcase then John Dillinger or Jesse James could ever do with a gun and they don't even have to wear a mask.

Look at the Grunt and Dump law firm where Douche Bag Mary works and you'll see that representing freeloaders and trash is their specialty. Douche Bag is short on looks but I suspect that she has bent over on her desk a few times for compensation from her sexual predator client. By now she no doubt has a good understanding of where the wild goose goes.

Every now and then I offer a tid bit of information in order to help people in their lives. For instance if you're not banging your spouse then rest assured someone else is. The three little words that your wife doesn't want to hear when she's getting laid is "honey I'm home."

I'm not a big book reader but I have read interesting books like Tiger's Revenge by Claude Balls and Yellow Lake by I.P. Daily. My favorite movie which I've watched a dozen times is Deep Throat with Linda Lovelace. Let's face it people breed like flies and there's nothing to stop it. Some men and I suspect that most men if given the opportunity will lie to hell and back in order to get a strange piece of ass. Men are basically animals and will lie, steal, cheat and even kill to have sex with a woman, unfortunately there are a lot of house wives that can be had at the right time. When I was a young man residential houses were used as whore houses but in these days it's apparent that it's gone big time and large work out gyms are fronting as whore houses and are fertile grounds for sexual predators and horny married people for sex.

Regarding my question pertaining to the North Carolina state law where "information and belief" over rides proof I also wrote to the North Carolina State Attorney asking him if he could show me the law. I have been advised by the lawyer Robert Mays that the law permits him to use "information and belief" when he's unable to produce proof.

October 10, 2019

Dear Mr. Stein,

I hate to bother you but I've asked just about everyone a question and no one seems to be able to give me an answer.

Where does it state in the North Carolina state laws that when someone is unable to prove that a married couple is or has been divorced they only need "information and belief" and documented proof is not necessary.

For the court to use "hearsay and a biased opinion" of a person to deprive me of the state law "tenants by the entirety" makes a mockery of Due Process. The court had absolutely no proof, not one iota of proof that my wife of forty years were ever divorced and yet the court ruled that we were "tenants in common" and ordered the sheriff to auction off our home and personal property to pay the other party $125,000.00 within twelve days.

If you would be kind enough to send me the information regarding the state law that will accept "information and belief" over proof I would really appreciate it.

Yours truly,

Robert L. Elliott

The most effective way of destroying a person's life is to smear and lie about them. People have no problem in believing a lie which politicians depend on to survive. Most people enjoy hearing something derogatory about another person because it makes them feel better about themselves, you can always tell when certain politicians are lying because their jaw moves. That's the problem with most Democrats, it has gotten to the point that they can't distinguish the truth from a lie.

Like I've said before stupidity has no boundaries. It's just a fact of life we're all born ignorant but some people work hard as hell to become stupid. In a family one child can be smart as hell and the other child can be dumb as a rock. It runs throughout most families including my own.

The best example of being stupid is the fanatical group known as Antifa. Talk about ignorance these sorry bastards win hands down. This human waste destroys property and assaults innocent people because they disagree with their point of view. This trash needs to be met with gun fire and plenty of it. It's high time for the tree of liberty to be watered.

If disrespect and lawlessness continues in our country then it may be time to suspend the U.S. Constitution for five or ten years until law and order can be restored in our country. It has gotten to the point that people have gotten too much freedom. They interpret freedom as the right to do any damn thing they please. Well, some news for you assholes your freedom ends where my nose begins. Kicking ass was my specialty for twenty five years and I won't hesitate to start again if forced to.

It seems like we've lost the art of communication. Anytime you say something to someone half the time they don't even understand what you're saying. For example one day last week I stopped at a local tavern on the way home for a nice cold beer. When the bartender served me the beer he pushed a bowl of nuts in front of me to enjoy with my beer as he has always done. A few minutes later a nice looking lady came in and sat down next to me and ordered a beer. Being the gentleman that I am I pushed the bowl of nuts over to her and asked her if she'd like to eat my nuts and that's how the fight got started.

You can rest assured I will never ask anyone again if they'd like to eat my nuts. To this day I'm reluctant to even mention nuts when I'm talking to someone. Every time I turn around it's the same old story, no one seems to understand what the other person is talking about.

A bagboy at a grocery store was helping a lady by pushing her grocery cart across the parking lot when the lady told the young bagboy that she had an itchy pussy. The bagboy responded and told the lady that she'd have to point her car out to him because all of the Japanese cars look alike to him. Just another sad example of the break down of simple communication.

I never knew that I could love animals so much until I moved into a big city and observed human behavior. People can get shot or mugged just walking to the grocery store for a loaf of bread. Park your car in front of your house and someone will steal your car and anything else they can stuff into the trunk of it. When you leave the house you may as well leave the door open so the thieves won't have to break it down. For myself I love small children and animals everyone else can go to hell.

Considering what I've been through with in my life regarding lying ass lawyers and brain dead judges getting mugged and shot at is a piece of cake. I spent twenty five years on a police department watching one ass kissing contest after another. Promotional opportunities depended on whose ass you had to kiss because ability didn't mean shit. The only way you could get promoted and be assigned to a worth while position was to kiss the right ass. I never amounted to much on the department because I just couldn't bring myself to sticking my nose in someone's ass. It got so bad about not having enough minorities we had people on the department that didn't know the difference between road and rode. Some recruits were actually taking sixth grade reading and spelling classes.

Affirmative Action and incompetent supervisors that didn't know their ass from a hole in the ground destroyed the department's efficiency and changed the department from a kick ass to a kiss ass police department. Every ethnic group formed their clubs in the department. The blacks, Hispanics and women all organized and all of the white Anglo-Saxons were left wondering what the hell was going on. All of the clubs became active putting pressure on the director of the department because they wanted their piece of the pie. The blacks didn't waste any time in hiring lawyers and filing suit against the department for discrimination. I learned fast that any club or organization that has progressive in their name will no doubt be controlled by racist. Individuals that can't compete and want higher supervisory positions given to them.

There was a time that police officers only had to worry about being stabbed in the back by disgruntled citizens but now they get stabbed in the back by other police officers. It use to be us against them but now it's us against everyone. The feeling of family that officers had for defending each other and watching each others back went to hell and it became every man for himself.

It got so bad that I took it upon myself to unite the Anglo-Saxons by creating the "Professional Law Enforcement Association" known as PLEA for protection. The following is the Preamble to the Constitution of the organization.

We the members of the Metro-Dade police department, do hereby associate ourselves for the following purposes. To support and defend the Constitution of the United States and the state of Florida, to promote the cause of professional law enforcement and to seek justice and equality for all, to cultivate a spirit of fraternalism and mutual helpfulness among our membership, to provide legal assistance to those who are represented by the association, to expose injustices within the system, to re-establish high standards, pride and a sense of fair play in the hiring and promotional processes within law enforcement, to seek equality and to be once again recognized as a legitimate part of the system, to diligently strive to expose and eliminate discriminatory practices that erodes the basic principles from which all our freedoms are founded , to stop the alien tide racial quotas and preferential treatment before it destroys the traditions of skill and excellence and to cast off the predetermined destiny handed to all of us by the system.

Let it further be known, that the replacement of individual rights and opportunities by a system of statistical classification based on race, color, sex, culture or ethnic background is repugnant to the basic concepts of a democratic society. To ignore the qualities and abilities of the individual is to sacrifice the great potential for innovation, for creation and for superior leadership. The Professional Law Enforcement Association embraces the fourteenth amendment of the United States Constitution and seeks "equal protection of the law" as any other citizen of the United States.

We hereby dedicate ourselves to the mission of ensuring that the Constitutional concept of citizenship with all attendant rights and privileges will be henceforth embraced by all people regardless of their race, color, sex, religion or national origin.

This is what we believe in and will fight for until hell freezes over.

The End

When I formed the Professional Law Enforcement Association and wrote the preamble it was under extreme pressure from the department and radical groups within the department. All it takes for evil to prevail is for good men to sit on their ass and do nothing. The officers that I thought would support me and have my back were busy looking for a place to hide. They had kissed ass for so long they didn't want anything to do with me and my movement. When the chips are down you can always tell who the chicken shits are.

The worse thing that could have happened to the young people of our country was eliminating the mandatory draft. The military service taught them responsibility, made them grow up and taught them how to communicate with other people. Without the draft now they can spend their time sitting around on their ass with their friends smoking pot and drinking beer. Apparently they don't teach history or civics in high school anymore because you can ask one of them a basic question regarding the government and all you'll get is a blank and dumb look.

When I attended the United States Navy boot camp in a freezing Northern state I learned a lot about responsibility. I learned that I should never have a piece of gum in my shirt pocket during inspection because it cost me to stand at attention for four hours on top of a dumpster. I never complained about standing outside and guarding a clothes line in the snow half the night. During the day I attended gunnery classes and always marched for a couple hours on the grinder to stay fit according to our kick ass leader. Discipline was the rule of the day and you had better not forget it. During the first two weeks in boot camp I lost sixteen pounds and rest assured it wasn't from sitting on my ass.

Most young people that are going to college don't belong there because they don't have the intelligence to understand higher education. They never conquered high school and why they think they're ready for college is beyond me. They belong in a vocational school learning a trade and becoming a useful citizen.

In my home town of Asheville , North Carolina we have women sitting around half naked with their tattooed tits hanging out right in front of the police station. These sorry ass bitches give new meaning to the word ugly. Looking at them will definitely turn men against having sex with women. The police officers just stand around doing nothing about it because the city fathers don't think there's anything wrong with it. Downtown Asheville is the last place a responsible parent would want to take their children and expose them to such filth.

Then we have the C.A.V.E. people who are "Citizens Against Virtually Everything." They spend their time trying to erase our country's history. People have to look at our country's past through the lens of what was legal and acceptable at that time in history. Northern slave traders were going to Africa and bringing back ship loads of slaves to America to be sold to Southern plantation owners. The largest slave auctions in America were located in New York city and one of the largest slave owners in the South was a black man.

The civil war was a war for independence and it wasn't fought over the question of slavery as most uneducated think. The people in the North were getting damn tired of the war and President Lincoln had to issue the Emancipation Proclamation to renew interest in the war. John Wilkes Boothe really screwed up big time shooting Lincoln because Lincoln's intentions were to repatriate the slaves back to their families in Africa. Enough of the civil war for now because we don't want to confuse Sharpton too much.

What ever happened to the good old days when you could go to a department store and buy a television set. Then go home plug it in and watch television. Everything is cable now and everyone has to pay to watch television. My monthly bill to watch television is $190.00 and half the time you're watching nothing but commercials. Every time I turn on the television set I am flooded with commercials from different law firms seeking clients for the law suits against the weed killer Roundup. Between Roundup and Johnson and Johnsons baby power it's a miracle that all of us aren't dead. They now claim that Johnson and Johnson's baby talcum powder causes cervical cancer. Well, here's a news flash for the medical community. Women have been sprinkling the baby powder on their muffs for more years then I can count which we can all agree.

I've been a muff diver since I was a teenager and many more men of my ilk are presently dying of throat cancer which should tell you something about what causes it. It doesn't take a rocket scientist to figure out what causes throat cancer. Many times after saying good night to a date I've left their place with a white powdery face and a smile. In those days I never dreamed that I was eating something that might be the death of me. If it happens so be it at least I'll die a happy man. I can't think of a better way to go.

As the cover of the book says "America's First Lady was underneath the desk in the oval office taking care of business while the Second Lady was out walking the dog," That must have been one fine tasting cigar that Bill was chewing on and it's a shame her pretty blue dress got stained. It reminds me of the story about the bridge builder. He built bridges his entire life and was never known as a bridge builder. He sucked one cock and he'll always be known as a cock sucker for the rest of his life.

Just a reminder, be nice to all the people you pass on your way up the ladder of success because you're going to meet the same people on your way back down. Don't tell your friends everything you know because they will know all your business plus what they know of themselves which will make them a lot smarter than you. People will judge you by the way you talk. Just listen and don't talk and they'll think you're intelligent as hell.

Regarding television commercials, I don't know how you feel about it but I get sick and tired of having to watch the same commercials over and over. Modern technology can do things today that that would have seemed impossible when I was a kid. Someone could be an instant billionaire if he would invent a simple little plug in device to plug into the wall socket with the television set to delete commercials. No doubt almost everyone owning a television set would buy one. Just my opinion and you know what they say about opinions. They're like assholes everyone has one.

Seeing and hearing Democrats like Schiff, Pelosi and Biden has done wonders for my constipation problem. Every time they talk it makes me want to have a bowel movement and at least it proves that they are good for something. Maybe it will change as they continue to campaign but right now it looks like the top four candidates running for president on the Democratic ticket is a wild haired communist, a make believe Indian, a cock sucker and a crook. Surely there must be someone some place that's worth while.

Considering the state that our country is in with millions of citizens walking around with their heads up their ass trying to recycle nothing surprises me anymore. It reminds me that there's a time to laugh and a time to cry. A time to be happy and a time to be sad but most of all a time to live and a time to die. The tree of liberty needs to be watered from time to time with the blood of patriots and it's high time to water it.

I was told that my next door neighbor loves eating a pussy and it literally scared the hell out of me. I thought there goes the neighborhood. Now I can't let my dear little pussycat run loose in my yard in fear that my pussy eating neighbor might catch it and eat it. I didn't waste anytime telling my wife to keep our cat indoors because our neighbor loves eating a pussy. I couldn't believe what I was hearing and almost fell over when my wife said that there wasn't anything wrong with eating a pussy and almost all men do it. I suppose next she'll be telling me that it's okay to eat our dog.

Until we get term limits for people serving in congress our country will remain in a state of conflict. A person can be elected and spend the rest of his or her life in congress doing nothing but sitting on their ass drawing a big pay check. Every time you turn around they're on some kind of two week break. Joe Biden was elected to the senate when he was twenty nine years old. Why is it that a president can only serve eight years in office and a senator or representative can serve until hell freezes over? I can understand why a United States Supreme Court Justice can serve a life term but even at that we have had and still have a justice that should have left office years ago. We've had people sitting on the bench drooling all over themselves in a wheel chair and when it came time to vote on something someone would hold the drooling person's hand up.

We have one Democrat running for president that can't remember what state he's in when attending a rally. No wonder that every lawyer wants to be elected to the senate. Where else can a person become a millionaire sitting on their ass doing nothing? A few years back I happened to be standing in front of a lawyers office and a lawyer happened to walk outside. Just for information I asked the lawyer how much it would cost to contest a divorce proceeding? He told me that it would all depend on the circumstances. Being polite I asked him if I owed him anything for the question and without hesitation he replied that will be seventy five dollars. Can you believe that? Seventy five dollars for taking no more than fifteen seconds of his time.

The Democrats bitch and object to everything that President Trump does and the Speaker of the House just stands around with her finger up her ass doing nothing to help our country. I understand that when she was a young woman she won the title of "Miss Grease Rack." Looking at her today it certainly looks like she's had her rack greased a few times. She's lost total control of the House of Representatives and now it appears to be controlled by the so called squad that consist of four flaming ass radicals.

If the Democrats think things are bad now for their far left radical beliefs wait until their beloved Supreme Court Justice Ruth Ginsberg finally kicks the bucket. When President Trump appoints another conservative to the court all the liberals will literally shit in their pants. They will try again to stop the person from getting on the court because they're scared to death that Roe vs Wade will eventually be reversed and the genocide of unborn babies will be stopped.

I've said it before and I'll keep saying it until hell freezes over. Any female considering an abortion and killing her unborn child should be required to go to a medical examiner's office and look at the perfectly formed unborn babies preserved and floating in mason jars. It will give pregnant women the opportunity to see the living human being that they are going to murder. If you think that's bad then look at the Governor of Virginia. That asshole believes in infanticide and thinks nothing of killing a baby after it has been born if the mother decides that she doesn't want it. The asshole even says that they will make the baby comfortable until the mother decides. Hopefully that murdering son of a bitch and the baby's mother will burn in hell where they belong. The best part of the governor apparently ran down his mother's leg when he was being conceived.

Since 1973 when murdering unborn babies became quite legal there have been sixty million babies murdered. A word of advice to the ladies that don't want to get knocked up, keep your legs closed and use your head if you can't resist the passion and temptation of sex.

I love and adore small children and animals but once the kids grow up into adults most fall into one of two categories ignorant and stupid. Some think absolutely nothing about lying, cheating, stealing and even killing another person. I personally don't trust anyone because I know the evil that lurks within a man's soul and heart. A life long friend won't hesitate to throw you underneath the bus if it's to his advantage to do so.

Have you ever wondered why some people seem to be smarter and more intelligent than other people? I'll let you in own something but if you accept it as a medical fact people will label you as a racist and bigot. Awhile back a study was conducted to understand why some people are more intelligent than other people and to find the answer to the question. Two very young children of different ethnic backgrounds were placed in the same exact environment to observe the development of each child. After the study was conducted it was apparent that one child was more intelligent than the other child. It was concluded that the only explanation was purely genetics. It was simply in one child's genes and not the other. Of course if you accept the logical conclusion of the study you'll be labeled as a racial bigot but the fact remains that genes effects the level of a person's intelligence whether you agree with it or not.

Never in the history of our country has a president ever been treated so unfairly as President Trump. The Democrats will not and have not ever accepted the fact that President Trump won the election. If crooked Hillary had won the election we would never have known how corrupt our leaders are. If President Trump farts the Democrats will form a committee and try to impeach him.

At present we have the workers at General Motors and the Chicago Teachers Union on strike for higher wages and benefits. I belonged to the Communication Workers of America for years and have a full understanding how union leadership can blow smoke up the workers ass. At one time I went on a seventy two day strike and when it was over we got the exact same thing that was offered to us on the first day we went on strike. For the most part the days of the unions have just about died. There's one thing that union members should realize when salaries go too high in a company one of two things will happen. Workers will be laid off or the working hours will be reduced to below thirty hours causing the workers to lose health benefits on top of less income.

Sometimes we have organizations like the American Civil Liberties Union bitching and objecting to everything doing with strict law enforcement. President Trump wants to get the DNA of all the immigrants coming into our country and of course the squawking starts from all liberal quarters. I'll go further than that and everyone can squawk until hell freezes over for all I care. Every human being within the borders of our country including anyone coming into our country or visiting should have their DNA and finger prints taken and entered into a national data bank. Every baby born in our country should have their DNA taken at birth and their finger prints taken before entering grade school.

What the hell has happened to patriotism? President Trump has asked everyone to hire American and buy American but it appears that the so called patriotic citizens couldn't care less about buying American. When you're out driving around make note of how many foreign vehicles are on the road around you. You'll discover that eight out of ten vehicles on the road are foreign made. It appears that the patriotic Americans are doing everything that they can do to destroy the American Automotive Industry. Some will show their patriotism by sticking an American flag decal on the bumper of their Japanese car.

The longer I live the more I dislike Hollywood trash that think they're better than the average citizen. Some of the assholes have played roles of being a bad ass for so long that they actually start to believe that they're mean and bad. Most of the women that you see and hear are nothing but washed up has beens that respectable men don't want anything to do with. Most of those particular women were conceived by only part of the male donor's sperm because most of it ran down their mother's leg.

The more I see of how corrupt our federal government had become under the Obama leadership the more I have a desire to move back to that pathetic little town in Alabama. I would rather live in poverty and have nothing than being subjected to the corrupt big city life. They always say that we're a nation of laws and as far as I'm concerned we're choking to death on laws.

Almost everyone you see on television holding a position of authority in the media or some company is a lawyer. Lawyers run the country by occupying every political office they can get and most couldn't care less if they destroy the country or not. Don't take my word for it, look at the Democratic House of Representatives and you'll understand what I'm saying.

Like I've said before if you're happy where you're living stay there. I lived in a beautiful house on top of a mountain ridge and for some unknown reason I got a bug up my ass and decided to move. I lived on five and a half acres and didn't have any close by neighbors to bother me. Moving was one big mistake that I've always regretted because now I find myself completely surrounded by nosey ass neighbors who don't know how to mind their own business.

One neighbor is paranoid as hell and thinks he's the high sheriff of the community. He's so hateful he even hates himself and his own family. He will do whatever he can to aggravate and piss people off. I use to work in a mental ward and I know a looney tune when I see one and this hateful prick needs mental therapy and plenty of it on top of lots of medication. If that's not bad enough I have another fat ass and nosey neighbor across the street that thinks she's a real bad ass and another Ma Barker. She operated a failed business for years with her head up her ass until she finally had to give it up and admit that she didn't know her ass from a hole in the ground about running a business. The first time I met her regarding a mistake her surveyor had made I realized that I was dealing with a moron. She immediately told everyone in the neighborhood that I didn't know who I was dealing with. A fart in the wind would have impressed me more than her big mouth. She was always a know it all and big mouth but no one has seen her around for the last couple months. With any luck maybe she got run over by the bus that she was always trying to throw me under.

Then I have neighbor number three on the right side of me. I sort of liked him but as time passed he showed that he had no balls and was controlled by his wife. I had installed a nice flag pole in my yard displaying a Confederate and Florida flag which his wife objected to. She wasted no time in telling her husband to come to my house and tell me to either move my flag pole or take down my Confederate flag because she didn't want to see it. Her wanting the flag removed reminds me of that old medical term tough shit.

Of course the flag still flies and I installed another flag pole that displays Old Glory and a Trump flag underneath it. This must really piss them off because they had Obama stickers plastered all over their cars. His nosey and controlling wife would take pictures of everything I was doing on my property and send them to my other pain in the ass neighbor Ma Barker. I finally told her to mind her own business and I haven't seen her since. Apparently she lost interest in taking pictures of my property and spends more time taking care of her own business. Her husband planted numerous trees in a dedicated roadway next to my property in an effort to hide my beautiful Confederate flag but it didn't work out.

I spent five hundred thousand dollars building a beautiful plantation style house and now I find myself in the middle of a sea of pricks so take my advice don't move. The more I think about it the more I'm inclined to go back to that little town in Alabama. A place where people help each other and say good morning instead of telling you to go to hell. Where a neighbor will help you to build a barn or plow a field when he sees that you need help. In those days back in the country families had a lot of children that would grow up and be able to help the parents with the work on the farm. The farmers for the most part were unable to hire people to help them with the farm work because no one had any money to speak of and it was a necessity to have large families.

Again it seems like everyone on Fox News and most appearing as guest on the show have written books concerning our country's political state of being in the world. Books that are so complicated it's almost too difficult for the average reader to understand. Quite frankly I'm sick and tired of hearing about the Middle East shit hole countries and their problems. They've been killing each other for hundreds of years and it shouldn't concern America.

All anyone has to do is write a book about the Arabs killing each other in some shit hole country display it on Fox News and within a week it will be advertised as a New York Times best seller. Every book that I've written is in simple language for the common reader to understand. Fiction people and stories is not my bag because make believe stories and people don't add any degree of intelligence to a person.

During my long life I've discovered that most men are like dogs. The ones that become lawyers represent the worse of society. When you get screwed to high heaven by one you'll understand why their profession is repugnant to me. It may be news to most people but 51% of the lawyers in congress are millionaires. No doubt it's because 84%

of the people in congress are lawyers sitting on their ass figuring out how to get more money and become rich like the other 51%.

At last we have a President Trump that has got his shit together, knows how to kick ass and the best thing going for him is the fact that he's not a money grubbing lawyer. He's a business man and the assholes in congress don't know how to deal with him. He doesn't even take his $400,000.00 salary but of course you will never hear any Trump hater and Democrat say anything about that including anyone with the news media.

How can anyone object to President Trump getting our country out of the never ending stinking senseless wars in the Middle East. We have spent seven trillion dollars in various shit hole countries at the cost of many American lives and for what? President Obama got us into a war by drawing his red line in the sand and then discovering that he didn't have the balls to enforce it. Between that and sending a plane load of money in the amount of over one billion dollars to Iran was the straw that broke the camel's back.

Let's face it every city that is run by liberal Democrats has fallen into ruin and chaos. During the Obama administration our country fell into chaos just like the big cities because of the same reason. The saving grace for America was when Donald Trump came down that escalator in the Trump Tower and stated that he was running for president of the United States.

Actually the way I look at the Arabs continually killing each other is that it provides a cleaning effect for their over populating society. They apparently don't think anything of killing each other and it's a good way of controlling their population since no one there apparently never heard of condoms. The last thing you'd want to be in their country is a condom salesman because you'd starve to death for sure. I personally don't give a rat's ass if they kill each other until there's no one left. It seems like they prefer riding a camel than driving a car so leave the happy people alone.

Mark my words because the day will come and it seems to be closer by each day for Plato's prediction to come true. Our country had become so corrupt that it's beyond belief. If crooked Hillary had won the election we would never had known how deep the corruption ran. When President Trump first started running for the presidency he stated that the entire system was rigged and he sure as hell knew what he was talking about. Even now, look at the sham being conducted by a bunch of Democratic morons calling for an impeachment of the president. Bare in mind that ignorance and stupidity have no boundaries and you can try to reason with a moron until you turn blue in the face and you'll never change their mind anymore than you can effect the tides by pissing into the ocean. They're stuck on stupid and it's a known fact that you can't fix stupid.

At present the Democratic Party doesn't have anyone worth while running for president and of all laughable things the born loser Hillary is thinking about jumping into the race again. She still hasn't gotten over someone knocking her out of the First Lady's position by being underneath the desk in the Oval Office taking care of business while she was out walking the dog. It's a shame that the First Lady got her pretty blue dress stained and I can only imagine how nice that cigar tasted. It must have been humiliating as hell being the Second Lady. I've also played second fiddle a few times in my life and I know the feeling.

If anyone thinks that being a police officer is a gravy job then join up and get your mind straightened up. I was a police officer for twenty five years and it didn't take me long after joining up to go back and check the job description to see if getting my ass kicked was in the job description. That's when I decided that if some punk assaulted me again I'd unscrew their head and kick their sorry ass. I learned to lower myself to their level so we could understand each other. There were times that I literally had to fight for my life. It became apparent to me that if I continued to rush into fights and hazardous situations I might not live long enough to retire. After giving it a lot of thought and since I only had one more year to retire I decided not to expose myself to dangerous situations anymore than I had to. 1 decided that if I was going to be shot and killed it would be in a donut shop. In my final year before my retirement I had three officers shot and killed on Miami Beach while investigating a possible auto theft. The last year before retiring Dade County Florida had 600 homicides. We would go out on a Sunday morning and collect the dead bodies left over from a Saturday night. It was nothing to find a body along the highway or in a vacant lot. I'll never forget the one in a vacant lot because the homicide detective looked at him and stated "the way he's dressed he could have danced all night." It gets to the point after seeing so much death it simply doesn't bother you anymore.

When I was a young kid I was a pain in the ass just like any other kid. One day a couple of us decided to take a break from working in the corn field and enjoy a watermelon from the adjacent watermelon farm. The only thing between our corn field and the watermelon field was a river about forty feet wide. That presented no problem because my uncle always left his row boat tied up at the corn field side for days that he wanted to go fishing. We took the boat and went over to help ourselves to a couple nice looking watermelons when suddenly two men appeared out of the woods and started chasing us. My friend took off running like hell and took our row boat back across the river to avoid getting his ass kicked by the owner of the watermelon patch. He was apparently just as scared as I was and didn't wait for me to get into the boat. That was the day that I learned to swim. I had an immediate choice to make, either swim or get my ass kicked. I discovered that the threat of getting your ass kicked was a great motivator to learn how to do something that you've never done before. To my surprise I actually beat my friend in the boat across the river. Needless to say I lost my taste for watermelon because it always reminded me of how close I came to getting my ass kicked.

Sometimes I'd sneak and drink some of my Uncle Tidy's home made grape wine and get shit faced. I was just a dumb ass farm boy that was growing up and experiencing life. I picked up the bad habit of smoking but never had any money to buy cigarettes so I had to improvise. I'd roll cigarettes made from dried corn silk or I'd smoke cross vine that grew in trees. When I wanted something to chew on in place of gum I'd just pull a little bit of tar out of a barrel that was left over from fixing the roof and chew on it. Our family being so poor it's a wonder that any of us survived.

Watching my mother I was taught things that I have never forgotten. Watching her kneeling beside the bed at night and asking the Lord to have his Guarding Angels watch over her boys in the navy and bring them safely back home. She always ended her talk with Jesus by saying the following prayer. "Now I lay me down to sleep I pray the Lord my soul to keep. If I should die before I wake I pray the Lord my soul to take." I only wish that I could have been a better Christian so everyone could have known how much I love Jesus. Hopefully he'll forgive me for my sins and make me a better person.

My mother always treated me like I was something special and when talking to someone she would always say that I was her baby boy. I would give everything I own and have if I could only hug mom one more time and tell her how much I love and miss her. A word of advice for everyone. Never fail to tell your love ones that you love them. Never say anything in anger to a loved one because if they die you'll regret what you said for the rest of your life. Some people actually find it hard to tell a loved one that they love them which I simply can't understand.

TO HELL AND BACK!

My family was dirt poor and lived under conditions that seemed completely hopeless. Being poor and having nothing can be a blessing some times. It exposes a person's heart and soul to other people and to himself. It builds a strong foundation for a person's life and the question of right and wrong will be forever engraved in that person's soul. According to the Bible it's easier for a camel to pass through the eye of a needle then for a rich man to enter the Kingdom of Heaven. Everyone will have to answer for their sins because there's no free rides into paradise.

The days of my life are surely numbered and hopefully when the time comes I will accept death gracefully and feel the presence of Christ. Hopefully when my soul leaves my body I'll be in paradise with the Lord and my family. You never know when your time is up on earth because the Lord never promised us one day of life and each day is a gift from him.

One night when I was the shift commander on the Sheriff's Department in Miami, Florida I had to literally fight for my life. I had assigned a plain clothes officer to an area that was plagued by a prowler. In the early morning hour the officer called for help and the dispatcher was unable to raise him on his radio which meant that he was in bad trouble. I responded to his location and saw that he was fighting a black male and I immediately ran to his aid. As we were trying to subdue and control the subject all of us fell to the ground at which time I broke my ankle as Officer Palmer yelled "Elliott he has my gun." As I tried holding his arm to keep him from shooting one of us he continued to shout " I'll kill your white ass." At that moment I saw Officer Tankersley running into the yard to assist us and took the gun out of the subject's hand. The subject was arrested and charged with resisting arrest with violence, aggravated assault, prowling and transported to the Dade County jail.

Approximately three weeks later the subject got shot and killed at the 167th street shopping center in North Miami Beach. It was learned that he worked there as a security guard and was trying to arrest someone for shop lifting when he got shot.

The captain that I worked for told me to escort his funeral since he was a security guard and I promptly told the captain to go ahead and write me up for insubordination because I wasn't going to escort his black ass any where. It would be a cold day in hell before I escorted the funeral of someone that tried to kill me.

There are some people that you can always tell when they're lying because their jaw moves. The Socialist Democrats have tried everything to over turn the 2016 presidential election and now they don't have anyone worth while running for president. It has gotten so bad and desperate that even crooked Hillary is thinking about running again. The most important thing on their agenda right now is that cows fart too much and we should do away with all the cows.

William Shakespeare had it right even in his time when he stated "the first thing we need to do is round up all the lawyers and get rid of them." No truer words could have been spoken. Lawyers will sue anyone for anything and if you don't believe it then fart on a crowded elevator and if there happens to be a lawyer in the crowd see how long it takes before you receive a subpoena to appear in court for violating a pollution law. You'll discover to your surprise that you violated the Environmental Protection Agency's law on pollution.

Sometimes everything about life can be amusing. Last week I was sitting in the waiting room at my doctor's office when a patient who had just been examined started to leave and dropped dead as hell before he got to the front door. The receptionist called back to the patient's doctor and told him that his patient just dropped dead in the waiting room as he was leaving. There was dead silence for a minute and then the doctor told the receptionist to turn his patient around and make it look like he was just coming in for his appointment instead of leaving.

Since I just had another birthday I'm glad that I went ahead and bought myself a funeral and grave site so I wouldn't end up in a dumpster behind Wal-Mart or some place else. The funeral home director was a nice fellow but it seem like he wouldn't agree with anything I suggested. I requested that my casket be covered with a Confederate flag and I be placed in my casket naked face down and the lower half of the casket lid be left open during the viewing so that my critics could kiss my ass goodbye. When they transport my casket to the cemetery that they also take a keg of beer for my love ones and last but not least that they have someone at the grave site singing "When the roll is called up yonder I'll be there." All my friends have assured me that they will decorate my grave with pussy willows because that's something I could never get enough of during my life. Of course there will be some smart ass that will stick a dildo into my flower vase to show everyone that I was a unforgiving prick.

When the Supreme Court Justice Ruth Ginsberg dies the Democratic Party will have a total shit fit because the thought of President Trump appointing another Supreme Court Justice would be too much to bear. Now we have a so called Republican that's nothing but a sore loser and jealous as hell of President Trump because he got elected as president. I can't believe that I actually voted for him when he ran for president and lost. After he lost and then started bad mouthing Trump I wasted no time in scraping all the Romney stickers off all my vehicles. He couldn't accept the fact that Trump became president and not him. To show how jealous he became he stated that if President Trump wins re-election in 20/20 he'll move out of the United States. I've heard that shit before from entertainers in Hollywood and all those assholes are still here. Apparently Mr. Romney thinks too much of himself and he's one sorry ass Republican. Hopefully the next time he runs for re-election the voters will kick his ass out of the senate. When he runs for re-election hopefully the voters will kick his ass out of the senate.

I love tomatoes but have found a good use for them besides eating. They're great for throwing them at some dumb ass politicians. Nothing can be more satisfying then hitting a liberal politician in the mouth with a ripe tomato when he's making a speech. It's high time for Republicans to fight back when they're harassed by loud mouth liberals in the Democratic Party. By now you're probably beginning to believe that stupid can't be fixed.

In the last seventy-five years the state of California has become a real third world country shit hole. The last few governors have done everything that they could do to destroy the place. They even made it a sanctuary state to hide and protect criminals from the federal agency ICE. They have thousands of homeless people living in tents and boxes along the roadways in town and they use the sidewalks and streets as their toilet. Feces and urine are all over the place which doesn't seem to bother the elected officials like Nancy, Maxine and the governor in the least. Some of the residents have had enough and at present thirty eight thousand people move out of the state each year. A beautiful state gone to hell because politicians didn't know their ass from a hole in the ground about administrating a government. Each year they permit the state to burn down because they're too stupid to require all power lines to be buried under ground. Wait until the right houses get burned down and then you'll see some changes made. For myself I feel more compassion for the poor animals and foul that get killed in the fires then I do for the people that voted for their asshole leaders.

Anytime you see the word progressive used in some organizations name or being used by some politician be placed on notice they're liberal as hell. It's always an indication that usually discrimination law suits will be coming down the pike. When a person can't compete they'll find some jerk ass liberal judge that will help them. It has gotten so bad now that a white person has to apologize for being white. One of the biggest assholes in America was John Brown, that got captured at Harper's Ferry by Robert E. Lee and they hung his sorry sick ass.

During the war for Southern independence, Robert E. Lee had to make a choice. He decided to leave the Northern Army and defend his home state of Virginia and the other Southern states in the Confederacy.

After the war it was decided by the North to bury dead Southern soldiers in General Lee's front yard which is now known as Arlington Cemetery. You can imagine why that was done. Doesn't it make you wonder why Robert E. Lee's mansion was never opened for the public to tour and see. President John Kennedy's grave is within eyesight of Lee's mansion and it's not on the list for the public to see.

There were 750,000 people killed in the civil war for Southern independence and now we have college morons destroying Southern statues. History loving and responsible citizens will finally get enough of the bullshit someday and there will be retribution to be paid. It never ceases to amaze me how ignorance seems to flow so freely in colleges. Maybe it's because they're taught by liberal jerk ass professors that don't know their ass from a hole in the ground.

Maybe my imagination is running away with itself again but it appears that almost every talk show host or politician that appears on television has written one or two books regarding our country's problems. If they appear on Fox News advertising their book within a week it will be advertised as New York Times best seller so they say. Most everyone on Fox News has written a book and has flooded the internet and book stores with books that are so involved and complicated that the average readers have trouble understanding them.

I'm still trying to figure out how they can get their books advertised on the internet with Barnes and Noble when an unknown author can't even get a mention from anyone, I constantly see silly ass books advertised on the internet for people to buy. People will buy anything if you get it advertised and out to the public. I have no doubt that some one could write a book on how to pick up a turd from the clean end and it would become a best seller in no time. Take my word for it, writing a book is a piece of cake and doesn't require anything special brain wise. Getting it advertised is the trick and it's expensive as hell so think about it before you get into writing.

My opinion regarding lawyers will never change. Apparently they're too damn lazy to work and that's why they became lawyers so they can sit on their ass and rake in the money from clients that don't know that they're being robbed. Every time I turn on the television there's always two or three law firms telling you to call them for a free consultation regarding the weed killer Roundup because you may be entitled to compensation if you ever used it. Some dipstick federal judge placed a two billion dollar judgment against the company because it can give people cancer. That wasn't bad enough now we have lawsuits against Johnson and Johnson because their baby powder gives women cervical cancer. Ever since I was a teenager women have sprinkled the baby powder on their muff and panties for hygiene purposes so they said.

There's an epidemic of men coming down with throat cancer and it doesn't take a rocket scientist to understand why. After making love to various women and girlfriends over the years it wasn't unusual for me to come up with a powdered mouth and face. At the time I didn't think anything of it but now if I don't come down with throat cancer it will be a miracle. Someday I'll probably be filing a law suit against Johnson and Johnson myself. Then of course the legal question will be argued regarding who is really at fault? Would it be Johnson and Johnson, the ladies that I loved or myself? Whatever the outcome I certainly don't have any regrets and wouldn't hesitate to do it all over again.

Considering that Jeffery Epstein use to fly big whigs and important people down to his private whore house in the Virgin Islands it makes me wonder why his death was so convenient. After looking at everything regarding his untimely death something smells rotten in Denmark. The prisoner that was in his cell with him was moved out to another cell. The two guards that were there to watch him just happened to be sound asleep. The cameras that viewed his cell and the hallway leading to his cell didn't work. He was suppose to be under suicide watch and he wasn't. A well known and highly respected doctor in the medical field went over the results of Epstein's autopsy and is of the opinion that the bones broken in Epstein's neck would indicate a homicide instead of a suicide.

There's no doubt that it was a good time for Jeffery Epstein to die otherwise there's a whole lot of important people got some explaining to do as to why they were making numerous trips to Jeffery's luxury whore house in the islands. Put it in the bank there's a lot of politicians running around nervous as hell with their hair on fire wondering when their name is going to come up. It's going to be fun to watch. Between that pretty little intern underneath the desk in the oval office taking care of business and Bill making trips to the islands with Epstein no wonder Hillary was grumpy as hell with the secret service agents. She could see that she was losing her position as first lady.

Some of the idiots running for president on the Democratic ticket can't keep their stories straight or too senile to remember where they're at or what they've said. I'm convinced that the Democrats would be better off if they nominated Mickey Mouse to run for president. At least Mickey would have more credibility then the rest of them. Rest assured the assholes will say anything to get a vote then they'll do as they damn well please once they get in office. President Trump is doing such a great job I'd be ashamed to admit that I was a Democrat.

Good old Joe he'll tell a crowd that he's against the Hyde amendment and having the federal government paying for abortions with taxpayers money leaving the impression that he's against abortions. He just found out that the Catholic church doesn't agree with his position regarding abortions. He's finding out that it's a real trick talking out of both sides of his mouth.

We have California burning down again like it does every year. The politicians don't do anything about it and won't until their houses start burning down. I've said it before and I'll keep repeating myself until someone starts to listen. Require that all the electrical wires are buried and they'll stop causing the fires. Everyone knows that when the high winds start the power lines sway and spark causing fires that destroy thousands of acres. I've seen interview after interview on television with California politicians regarding the fires and in my opinion they appear to be completely ignorant on how to stop the destruction. As I have said before the solution for stopping the destruction is simple as hell but apparently too difficult for the local politicians to understand. The politicians just stand around scratching their ass wondering why they have so many homeless people sleeping on the streets in tents and boxes. Has it ever occurred to them that to rent a place to live is impossible because the rents have gone so high they don't have the money to rent a place. Now the cities designate large parking lots for people to park their cars in and sleep in their cars. Anyone that owns a trailer or R/V can park wherever they please and set up house keeping. Living conditions in California has become so deplorable that thousands of residents leave the state each year looking for a better place to live.

When you get old as hell and find yourself standing at death's door you'll wonder about all the years and friends that filled your life. The things that you didn't do and should have done. Those things in your life that seemed so big at the time don't seem to be so important anymore. Standing at the edge of death will certainly clear a person's mind as to what his life must have meant to others. For myself I now realize that I would do things differently if I could live my life over again. My life has been one bumpy road with plenty of ups and downs that I still don't understand. My Christian teachings was to forgive people that offended me but my human weakness prevents me to forgive like the Lord teaches.

The ultimate example of forgiveness was when the Lord Jesus Christ was crucified on the cross, he stated "Forgive them father for they know not what they do."

No one would have ever known how corrupt our country was if Hillary had won the presidential election. President Trump was only in office nineteen minutes before one of the top newspapers came out with the headline " Now the impeachment of Trump begins." With that the entire news media excluding Fox News started a campaign to get President Trump out of office. The Democrats have tried everything they can think of to overturn the 2016 presidential election. All of the party leaders are running around with their head up their ass not knowing what to do. The Speaker of the House lost control of the party and now it's ruled by a bunch of nitwits that have destroyed the Democratic Party and what it use to stand for. Right now they seem to be having a contest as to who can give away the most free stuff. They can't get it through their thick head that nothing is free, someone has to pay for it.

The more I look back on my pathetic poor life in Alabama the more I appreciate living and growing up there. Things were bad and we didn't have anything but life seemed to be simple. When you work all day in a cotton or corn field in ninety degree heat it has a way of bringing you closer to your creator. I never realized what I would be confronted with when I grew up and moved to the big city and how complicated life could get to be.

If you still believe in the concept of Innocent until proven Guilty, Due Process and the Rule of Law then maybe you had better read the book Kangaroo Justice written by yours truly and wake yourself up to the actual truth to what's going on within our justice system. In my particular case you will discover that "information and belief" over rides actual proof which was supported by the Superior Court in Asheville, North Carolina. Under no circumstances should a court accept hearsay and a person's biased opinion over actual proof. That particular potted plant judge was wrong then and he's wrong today and he'll be wrong tomorrow.

Whenever you hear someone cursing and condemning anything that our country has done in the past don't jump to conclusions until you weigh what you're saying. I've pointed it out in the past and apparently it needs to be said again. What is considered wrong today was perfectly legal many years ago and practiced by upstanding and religious people. Slavery was an accepted practice for a thousand years including in our mother country England. Many nations accepted it as a way of life. Things that are quite legal and accepted today may well be illegal in the future so don't be too judgmental on our fore fathers.

It still continues and seems to be endless. Everyone that appears on television seems to have written a book regarding the political problems facing our country today. The authors gives their opinions and it has become so complicated that most readers can't understand and digest what's being said. The information in the books become a confusing web of finger pointing, allegations and accusations that jumbles a readers mind. One of the well known people that that appears on Fox News could easily write a book on why it could be an impeachable offense if President Trump happened to fart during a press conference. The Democrats would immediately form a committee and subpoena the entire White House staff as witnesses. All the Trump haters know that the only possible way of defeating President Trump in the next presidential election is to impeach him.

If you ever start thinking about writing a book take my advice and don't do it. It's simply not worth it in time and money. Writing is the easy part now try and get it published and on the market for people to see and buy. If you don't know how the system works and what it takes as an unknown writer to get noticed then you'll be dead in the water. It can be frustrating as hell when you see a well known author write about a reckless fart in an elevator and within a week it's advertised as New York Times best seller and proudly shown on Fox News with the author. If you think you could be so lucky to have your book advertised on television, on the internet and placed in book stores for the public to see then you're pissing into the wind because it won't happen. You're a nobody trying to break into a closed world that won't recognize you or your work.

When you get old and crippled the original meaning of life disappears and you begin to realize that you're suddenly standing at the door of death. Your idea of what should have been doesn't seem to matter anymore. Always try and live by the Golden Rule and treat people the way you want to be treated. I personally respect a thief more than a liar because a liar can literally destroy you. I had a lying ass female lawyer in Plantation, Florida do everything she could do to destroy my family and hopefully she'll meet an early end to her miserable life. It would make my day if I could hear of her demise. If that happens hopefully they will bury her face up with her mouth open because I intend to make her grave my personal latrine. That sorry bitch sued me starting back in 1998 and kept suing me until 2016. She had trailer trash for clients that gave new meaning to the word freeloader. The husband is a sexual predator and his ugly wife is a bonafide psychopath.

Finally someone has started to question the death of Jeffery Epstein. They're trying to make everyone believe that he committed suicide to save someone's ass. He was in the process of trying to get out of jail and he had 571 million dollars in assets. Anyone with that much money and in the process of obtaining a bus load of lawyers sure as hell doesn't commit suicide. Everyone knew that he was murdered but no one had the balls to say it until medical examiner Doctor Baden decided to tell it all on national television. Now the female television anchor on ABC has come out and told how ABC wouldn't permit her to expose how Epstein was operating a high class whore house in the Virgin Islands for well known political figures in America and even across the big pond to England. The truth is going to come out and boy is it going to be juicy.

The Democrats think that the impeachment bullshit is a big story. They haven't seen anything yet. It was obvious that Jeffery Epstein knew too much and he had to die before his operation broke wide open for everyone to see. There was just too much at stake and going to the Virgin Islands was easy as hell compared to getting a blowjob in the oval office. That's one cigar that I would love to smoke.

Now I see the brainless idiots in New York City are protesting and vandalizing property because they object to having to pay $2.75 to ride on the subway. They run up and down the streets yelling profanities at the police and vandalizing the police cars. Most are probably on some kind of welfare which has been going on for generations. The best way of stopping most of the morons from their violent behavior would be to cut off their supply of food stamps and all welfare when they are arrested for destroying property.

People have to understand why younger people act the way they do. The family as we know it doesn't exist in most black families. Too many young people don't even know their father. The father can usually be found at the local pool hall or some place else drinking the day away while the mother is out working some place trying to survive. That leaves the grand mother at home taking care of the kids. When the family unit is split then the kids run wild whenever they get the chance due to lack of supervision. Now you can call me a racist if it makes you feel better but what I've said is the damn truth whether you agree with me or not.

During my twenty five years with the Dade County Sheriff's Office in Miami, Florida I've attended a couple good riots myself and know what I'm talking about so don't try and blow smoke up my ass regarding riots. I've seen innocent people burned alive in their car and a young person being dragged out of his car and stomped on. Then run over by his own car numerous times until he was smeared up and down the street. He was an innocent young man that drove into the riot not knowing what was going on and it cost him his life.

Riots give the low life's of the community the opportunity to steal everything they can carry. If the merchandise they steal doesn't last long enough then they'll simply replace it during the next riot. It's a simple way of life, why work and buy something when you can steal it. The way water cannons are used these days to break up a riot is a waste of time and good water. The best way of dispersing an unruly crowd is to use the water cannon supplied with raw sewage from septic tanks. Then let's see some loud mouth protester stand there with his or her mouth open cursing the police.

One thing about the criminal justice system that sucks big time is the Parole Boards. There is no justification for any Parole board. A Parole Board is nothing but a magnet for corruption and bribery. If a person is sentenced to a term in prison then he or she should have to serve everyday of it. If the person causes problems and disrupts the jail operation then simply add more time to their sentence. With a Parole Board a prisoner can simply be bought out of jail with a bribe. The prisoner doesn't need a hacksaw to saw his way out of jail when he can buy his way out.

We have governors today that are releasing hundreds of prisoners out of prisons because the prisons are over crowded and it will save the state money. My solution would be to build more prisons not to reward criminality. An officer administering some roadside justice to a disrespectful punk is completely justified and should be an accepted procedure. As I've stated before when I was on the police department getting my ass kicked was so routine that I finally checked the job description to see if it was actually part of the job description. I decided right then that my ass wasn't going to be used anymore as a football for the public's entertainment.

Why some men grow beards is beyond me. I suppose there could be many reasons but they escape me. First I don't trust a man with a beard because right away I think he's hiding his face for a reason and I always feel that the main reason is that he doesn't want someone to recognize him for some crime. Besides that a beard is dirty as hell and trying to eat with hair hanging all over your face would certainly present problems. A woman kissing a man with a beard would be like kissing an armpit. Most of all it amazes me that a man will cultivate hair on his face that grows wild on my ass.

My life has been one mountain after the other and especially the day that a medical doctor told me that my one and only teenage son had a brain disease that there was no cure for and that he would never get well. It completely crushed my heart and soul. At that moment I lost my zest for life and nothing seemed to matter anymore. I fell into a deep state of depression and could understand why some people don't care about living life. The world could have come apart and destroyed itself for all I cared. Yes, I cried every day and every night as I prayed and begged the Lord to help my son get well. I would have given my life in a heart beat if it would help my dear son. It seemed like my reason for living had been taken from me.

We're not suppose to understand God's plans because in time they will be revealed to each one of us. Someday I will understand why my son became sick. The Lord has a way of changing the direction of your life. The other night I was listening to the preacher Joel Osteen and he said to never give up when things are going bad because the Lord will open a new door for you and show you better times. It struck home with me because of all things he mentioned book writing and said to never give up because a new door will be opened for you. I know that I'm standing at the door of death and when I pass through it I know that my Lord will be with me to comfort me.

People always say "If there's a God then why does he permit geno-cides to happen like in Nazi Germany? Here's a news flash for the close minded. God doesn't control the events that happen on earth. People were born and given Free Will and only people themselves dictate the events on earth. I personally feel that whatever happens on earth is simply an "accident of existence" so don't blame the Lord for people killing each other.

A good example of how much the media knows is when the Time magazine put Adolph Hitler on the cover of their magazine in 1939 and called him the man of the year and within months he invaded Poland. All the ignorant assholes in America supporting the Socialist Democratic Party should be reminded that Adolph Hitler was a so-cialist. If you're running for public office and especially for a seat in Congress promise all the voters that if you get elected everything will be free. Attack the rich because all free loaders resent wealthy people. Tell the voters that everyone will get a brand new automobile of their choice and you'll win by a landslide.

For myself I don't believe anything I hear and about half of what I see. Apparently I don't know much about cars since they've started importing so many different makes from different countries. I had a nice looking woman tell me last week that she had a nice itchy pussy and I thought that she was referring to her Japanese car.

Nothing pisses me off more then to see someone waving the American flag and proudly singing God bless America and when it's over go outside and drive off in their Japanese car. Of course they usually stick a decal of the American flag on the bumper of their car to show their true blue patriotism.

At present Toyota stock is on the Dow Jones at $135.00 a share, General Motors at $39.08 a share and Ford listed at $9.10 a share. Doesn't this tell you what's happening to the American Automotive Industry? The person buying a foreign car couldn't care less about American companies going broke and it doesn't mean anything to them that thousands of American workers will be put out of work. I'll be damned if I'm going to hurt the American worker and support Japan over America.

That's the way it is with law and order. Someone will advocate and support strong law and order until it effects them. When I was on the police department one individual kept complaining and calling the department about people speeding on his street. I was sent there to enforce the traffic laws and the first speeder I caught was the one making all the complaints.

No doubt you're one of those people that still believe in the concept of "innocent until proven guilty." Later on I'll go into a story about that subject which you will find hard to believe but rest assured it actually happened. The complete story was written in the book Kangaroo Justice but I'll briefly go into it later on so you'll be able to understand how easily the courts can blow smoke up your ass in the name of justice.

Looking at all the candidates running for president on the Democratic ticket disgust the hell out of me. I'm about as excited as finding a turd in the punch bowl at a family gathering. I have never witnessed such a bunch of idiots running for president in my entire life. All of the morons support Socialism and are apparently ignorant that Adolph Hitler was a Socialist. The young people in high school and college have no understanding of Socialism and for some strange reason they think everything is free under Socialism. The word free is misunderstood by most people because nothing is free. Someone has to pay for every free thing you enjoy.

The so called impeachment inquiry being conducted by the Democratic Party shows how desperate the Democrats have become. It appears that their star witnesses don't know their ass from a hole in the ground and the entire hearing is nothing but a political sham that holds no water. Regarding their witness former Ukraine Ambassador Yovanovich, she is nothing but a fired and disgruntled ex-employee with an axe to grind. Now she can spend her time in the kitchen baking cookies and being useful to someone that appreciates her.

Have you ever had to literally fight for your life? Well 1 have and it changes your outlook on life. It will test your ability to forgive someone. I discovered that there are some people that place no value on life and think absolutely nothing of killing another person. Just to make my point it doesn't seem to bother some women to kill an unborn child by having what they call an abortion which is just another word for murder. In my humble opinion there's a lot of flaming ass liberal people that should have been aborted because the country would be better off without the assholes. If the Democrats think they have problems now just wait until the Supreme Court Justice Ruth Ginsburg kicks the bucket and President Trump appoints someone else to take her place on the court. The liberals will lie to hell and back in their effort to block anyone that President Trump appoints.

As for myself ever since my retirement from the police department I've lived most of my life being thrown underneath the bus. I've had the best of them throwing me underneath the bus, lawyers, judges, trailer trash and church goers. When you're under the bus it doesn't matter who the hell put you there. If you're going to survive expect the hard times and try your best to live with it. When you fail get back up, brush yourself off and tell the onlooking bastards to get out of your way.

If you'd like to experience failure then write a book. Unless you're a well known person your chances of being a successful author is about as good as being a snowball in hell. A well known author can write about anything underneath the sun and within a few days it will be advertised as a best seller all over the internet. Writing is the easy part getting it on the internet and in stores for people to see and buy is the tricky part. Maybe it's my imagination working overtime but it seems like everyone on Fox News has written a book and almost all of the guest that appears on their show. Most of the male host has written a book or two regarding the political situation confronting our country today. If you read all of their books you'll get confused as hell because the average reader can't digest all the information being thrown at them. Between all of the books you have a truck load of opinions and you know what they say about opinions they're like assholes everyone has one.

If I wasn't so damn old and crippled I'd try and make it back to that old run down farm in Alabama where people are civil to one another. The big city sucks and you can get shot for blowing your horn at someone or get mugged walking to the store. I strongly recommend that anyone living in a big city disconnect their car horn to prevent them from accidently blowing it.

The last year that I worked on the Dade County Sheriff's Office we had six hundred homicides. After a weekend it wasn't anything to find a corpse lying beside the roadway or in a vacant lot. After a wild weekend the last one that I came upon was really dressed fancy and must have danced the night away until someone shot him and left him in a vacant lot.

Parents and people in general just don't get it. The colleges are packed with people and especially young people that don't have any business attending college. Simply put most don't have the intelligence to understand things on the college level. If you doubt what I'm saying then ask some high school student to name the three branches of government and they'll give you a dumb look because they have no idea what the hell you're talking about.

One good example of what I'm talking about occurred at the recent Harvard and Yale football game. Hundreds of students ran out onto the football field and stopped the game from playing so they could protest that our government was destroying our country by using fossil fuel, driving cars, flying airplanes and raising cows because they fart too much and it pollutes the atmosphere. Talk about ignorance they win the trophy for stupidity hands down and they attend well known colleges.

For myself I've never seen such a display of gross ignorance and I have a news flash for the morons. There are almost seven billion humans on earth and they fart a damn sight more than a bunch of cows. If all the humans should fart at the same time and someone strike a match the earth would explode. Humans breed like flies so don't start putting blame on the innocent cows.

It seems like almost everyone spends their time wishing that they had more in life and don't appreciate what they have. It seems like they're always wishing for something better. Well take my advice and get over it. Wish in one hand and shit in the other and see which one gets filled first. When I was on the police department I created the perfect organizational chart of the department which was recognized and approved of by all my subordinates. I placed and arranged piles of cow feces on the wall to represent the people running the department. I was never considered for upper management because I was too opinionated and thought that it was wrong to play golf on county time. It was decided by the section supervisors that I just wouldn't fit in and would cause problems.

The only thing I ever saw those particular upper management personnel do was getting drunk on their ass at the local Howard Johnsons and playing golf . Job security was defined as kissing someone's ass and being one of the good ole boys. I have a strict rule of not kissing anyone's ass so I didn't fit in with the good ole boys club. By the insiders the department was a picture of corruption and true friendship had no value. Your friend today may well be your biggest enemy tomorrow. I never really faced corruption until I worked for an ass kissing captain in the Northwest District Station. This asshole was more interested in being popular with the black culture then enforcing the law. He was such an ass kisser he would call a subordinate into his office and belittle him in front of community leaders that he had invited into his office. I lost all respect for him and as far as I was concerned he was nothing but a jerk and would have been more suited working at Burger King.

Everyday it seems like I hear and see someone being stupid. I always have to remind myself that we all were born ignorant but some work real hard to be stupid and as you probably know it's impossible to fix stupid. I'm totally convinced that there is a relationship between intelligence and genetics. It's an indisputable fact that some cultures are more intelligent than other cultures. If you subscribe to this true fact then be prepared to be labeled a racial bigot by some moron that proves your point.

Beware of any organization that uses the word progressive in their name. It usually indicates that they're out to file discrimination lawsuits against everyone. They routinely investigates police departments and businesses to see if blacks are in upper management positions, if they don't see enough blacks in those positions they inform the companies and departments of their intention to file lawsuits. The companies will always pay them to settle the case out of court rather then go to the expense of going to court. It's plain and simple extortion but it works every time. Jesse Hairlip has been doing it for years and made a good living doing it.

Contrary to popular belief being old as hell doesn't automatically make you senile and stupid. I'm old as dirt and I'll still match my level of intelligence with any of the sorry bastards in congress. Doesn't it strike you strange that 51% of the people in congress are millionaires? The Democrats really have their problems to worry about. Supreme Court Justice Ruth Ginsberg had to go back into the hospital with a fever and chills. This liberal old bat was going to retire but when Trump got elected president she decided not to retire and prevent President Trump from appointing another conservative to replace her. Well dear old lady President Trump is going to be elected again in 20/20 and considering your poor health you'll never live long enough to deny him another appointment to the court.

Anyone that still believes hat a person is innocent before the law until proven guilty had better wake up. You can believe it or not but in my particular case as I have mentioned the court didn't require any proof in order to find me guilty. It was ruled by the Superior Court judge in Asheville, North Carolina that the only thing required to find someone guilty is "information and belief" that something occurred and actual proof is not necessary. The state was unable to produce one document of proof or one iota of evidence and yet I was convicted on hearsay and one person's biased opinion. I've written to everyone in the state of North Carolina in an effort to find out where it states in the law that "information and belief" over rides actual proof. It's disappointing as hell when a so called judge rules that proof is not necessary in order to find a defendant guilty. If you think that it can't happen then check the court records in Buncombe County North Carolina and seeing is believing.

My life has never been easy and it's just been one mountain after another to climb. Even when I rode motors on the police department. The department paid me twenty dollars extra each month for hazardous duty pay for riding motors. I was so damn broke I never carried more than twenty five cents in my pocket just in case the Royal Castle hamburger joint charged me for a cup of coffee. On many days I've sat next to a KFC wishing I had the money to buy myself a meal. I was only making $362.00 a month and that didn't go very far with my bills. I took an extra job at night working security at the Miami Drive Inn theater for seven dollars a night and was glad to get it.

I finally got promoted to sergeant and was assigned to the General Investigation Unit in the Detective Bureau. During the next few years in the role of a detective I went to different schools and obtained college degrees in an effort to better myself in the department. I soon discovered that education and ability wasn't considered for upper management positions. Promotions were simply based on who you know and if you would go along with the program whether you agreed with it or not.

When I was promoted to lieutenant I was assigned to the Shift Commander's Office and witnessed behavior by some detectives that turned my stomach but there was nothing that I could do about it because it appeared to be an accepted practice that had been going on for years. One kiss ass detective spent most of his time going to a motel with a police woman from another district while on duty. While he was banging her at least every week the sorry lying bastard accused me of leaving the station and using a county car. On numerous occasions I would see two or three detectives drinking at the Whale and Sail Bar until they were drunk on their ass then put in for overtime the next morning. We had one detective that had drugs of some sort in his bathroom ceiling which they could never find. Then we had one detective that wouldn't even report to work and stay home in bed and then turn in a work sheet that he worked all night. It was obvious to me that there was no discipline or control in the unit. Everyone did as they damn well please without question and I couldn't wait to get the hell out of the unit because it was hopeless. I tried to correct the situation and bring it to light but discovered that there wasn't a damn thing I could do about it. Defrauding the county and the lack of discipline had been going on for so long it was accepted and considered a tradition. The detectives weren't happy that I was in the unit and complained about my rules of conduct and of all things I was written up by my supervisor. That was the first and only time in twenty five years with the department that I was ever written up and criticized by anyone.

The married detective that was banging his girlfriend on county time was instrumental in having me written up because he spent most of his time kissing the captain's ass. I met some sorry ass officers but this asshole beats them all. In retrospect I should have told his wife about her husband's girlfriend. That sorry son of a bitch would lie about everything and swear it's the truth. If the truth was known he wouldn't make a pimple on a real man's ass. My supervisor should have never taken disciplinary action against me without confronting me first to see if it was justified and proper. The captain should have known better considering who was feeding him false information. One big jerk who thought nothing of cheating on his wife and getting all the ass he could get on county time.

Maybe my imagination is working overtime again but it certainly seems like the higher up the ladder of success a person goes the bigger asshole they become. When someone was promoted and assigned to a unit the first thing they would do is make changes whether it was needed or not. That was to let everyone know that a new person was in control and to show their authority. Usually the new supervisor didn't know shit from shinola about the operation and was assigned to the unit as a result of the "peter principle." For those who aren't familiar with the term "peter principle" it's a way of getting someone transferred to some other place because they didn't know what the hell they were doing in their present assignment.

A couple times in my life I thought that I might make it to the top of the mountain but that wasn't to be. I discovered that in everyone's life there was a time to be sad and a time to be happy. I've certainly had enough sadness in my life and hopefully the happy days are just around the corner. I had back surgery on January 22, 2015 and it left me crippled and unable to walk without a walker. Since that day my life has been one big bore and nothing seems to be that important anymore.

They all say that the best things in life are free. Well they had better add being able to walk to the list. Between two strokes, a heart attack and crippling back surgery it just about finished my life. The strokes effected the vision in my left eye and I'm unable to drive without taking a high risk of getting into an accident. The surgeon cut too many nerves in my lower back destroying the nerves in my right leg leaving it paralyzed from the knee down.

On top of everything else I have sugar diabetes and have to survive on pills. I have the usual health issues that come with old age and I know the feeling of standing at the door of death. Standing there and knowing that your life is coming to an end will make you ask the Lord if he will let you live a little longer so you can finish your plans. I've made numerous attempts in business and now even in book writing but the negatives in my life far out weigh the positives and failure will no doubt raise it's ugly head again. Sometimes I'm inspired by the preacher Joel Osteen and the other night he made a statement that hopefully I can live by. He stated if you are confronted with failure try harder and never give up because if you do fail it just means that the Lord is going to open a new and promising door for you.

Through all my disappointments and heart aches the one thing that finished destroying my life was when the unbelievable lawsuit was filed against me by the lying ass female lawyer in Plantation, Florida. Life is so uncertain and that sorry bitch will have to answer for what she has done to me before God Almighty. Her salvation on earth is the fact that I'm crippled and can't get around. That bitch wears perjury on her sleeve as a badge of honor and had to be doing a couple judges in Fort Lauderdale because she could get anything she wanted signed and issued. No doubt she spent a lot of time bending over while the judge showed her where the wild goose goes. Her husband who works in the same law firm must be dumb as a rock or just thankful that someone is banging her so he doesn't have to.

There are some good things that happened in my life that I will never forget like my first love and last love. I carried a picture of my first love in my billfold for sixty years and her memory is etched in my soul and heart. I fell in love with her while in high school and shortly thereafter she moved to Galveston, Texas. We would write to each other and I must have written at least a thousand letters to her at Gail Ackerman, 1218 Bayou Shore Drive Galveston, Texas. She would always write to me and print the letters S.W.A.K. on the envelope. She would always write "written with a pen and sealed with a kiss if you love me you'll remember this." Later in life I thought that I had located her on the internet but it was not to be. She had been a majorette at Miami Jackson high school and I was a student at Miami Edison high school when we met and I fell madly in love.

With all the heart breaks and disappointments in life sometimes I wonder if it's all worth it. As a teenager growing up in Miami, Florida it was just too short and having a broken heart was too long. Many times I thought that it would be nice to simply disappear. I discovered that your friends would abandon you for the slightest reason if you disagreed with them. As I grew older I simply ran out of friends and found out that life could be lonely as hell. I had one dear friend left and as we were having a cup of coffee he fell over dead without making a sound. With that and finding my dear mother dead on her living room floor I realized that with my life I was skating on thin ice.

As stated on the cover of the book you will notice that I have no confidence in the Rule of Law. If you still believe in the concept that you're "innocent until proven guilty" then you've never had an experience with the justice system or you simply don't know what the hell is going on. I was found guilty in a so called court of law without one document of proof or one iota of proof against me. If you think I'm crazy as hell then check the court records in the Buncombe County Courthouse in Asheville, North Carolina during October 2016. That particular potted plant judge ruled that proof wasn't necessary and "information and belief" over rides actual proof. The Superior Court judge never once even recognized that my wife and I were in the courtroom. If this is what they call justice then I want no part of it.

As far as I'm concerned lawyers and judges deserve less respect then used car salesmen. Apparently How to Steal 101 is a required course in law school. If you want to see wall to wall assholes look toward congress. They get paid $174,000.00 a year for doing nothing but sitting on their ass. It seems like they take a two week break every other month or so and since they work part time they should only be paid part time wages. The president can only serve eight years but senators can die in congress from old age. We have one running for president now that was elected to congress when he was twenty nine years old and he's pushing eighty years old now. We must have term limits in congress or our country will never get straightened out the way it should be. This particular senator doesn't even know where he's at half the time and constantly says shit that he doesn't know anything about. He's just one example why we must have term limits.

It's common knowledge by ordinary citizens that lawyers are basically thieves. Most lie so much they get where they can't tell the difference between a lie and the truth. Most of the lawyers and judges that I've dealt with over the years didn't know their ass from a hole in the ground. The day I have any respect for a money grubbing lawyer a piano will come out of my ass playing "who would have thought it."

If you still believe in the so called "Code of Silence" or what is known as "Privileged Communication" between a lawyer and his client then you've been asleep and don't know how lawyers interact with each other. When I hired a lawyer to protect my interest in a matter it didn't take me long to realize that he was spending more time talking to the opposing lawyer than to me. My lawyer did a piss poor job in representing me and appeared determined to throw me underneath the bus. When I asked him to depose some trailer trash people that were going to court against me he refused saying that it was too expensive. I was the one paying the bill so why did he object? For some reason I was getting the feeling that the fix was in. Plainly put I got where I didn't even trust my own lawyer.

Before moving to the big city I was raised to believe that there was good in all people which proved to be a false belief. The more I'm around city people the more I long to be back in Alabama on that broken down little farm picking cotton for a living. I've struggled my entire life trying to dig myself out of one hardship after another. I finally realized that the rut I always found myself in is nothing but a grave opened at both ends.

I guess you can call me a tree hugger because it bothers me to see forest fires and people cutting down beautiful trees. Take for example the beautiful seventy feet high and forty feet wide tree cut down to be used as a Christmas tree at the Rockefeller Center. The tree weighed fourteen tons and took many years to grow that big and shouldn't have been destroyed just for people to look at. When I see a forest fire and thousands of acres being burned I can't help but feel bad that all of the birds and animals are being killed. It's apparently a natural thing for humans to kill each other for any reason but animals seem to have a higher standard for living. I love all animals and small children but unfortunately children grow up and become their environment which is usually bad and determines what their behavior will be. My attitude toward most grow ups isn't complimentary and I usually prefer to stay alone and mind my own business and not be bothered.

When I was a young man in my teens I developed a interest in females just like everyone else. In those days the location of a whore house wasn't advertised for everyone to know. I'll never forget the first one I went to and seen all of the good looking women in the living room of the house waiting to be selected by a customer. I selected a beautiful looking red head and when we went into a room she asked me what would I like, being new to the world of love making I didn't know what to say so I told her to give me ten dollars worth which was a beautiful and wonderful experience in my life.

Now days it's free because the entire concept of a whore house has changed. It's no longer called a whore house even though it's recognized as one. It has gone public and big time in the form of spas and gyms located on main street for everyone to see. It's common knowledge that husbands, wives and anyone else looking for a strange piece of ass will join the health spa to meet people with the same desires. It's a popular hangout for sexual predators because it's wall to wall with half naked women in need. It always starts off with a sexual predator finding himself someone that will enjoy talking to him and within a few short days he will end the workout with telling the young lady let's have a cup of coffee. before long he'll have her in the local motel screwing her brains out and telling her how beautiful she is and how fortunate her husband is to have her. After he bangs her real good a few times she will be madly in love and give him money, flowers and even golden jewelry to wear. Usually the predator is nothing but a bum and a freeloader that doesn't work and survives by ripping off every welfare system that he can find.

America is my country tis of thee but most of the people in it can go straight to hell as far as I'm concerned. I've discovered that most human beings will keep you as a friend as long as it's convenient for him. Everything is wonderful as long as he finds out that you're just like him but let yourself be some one that he doesn't agree with and that will end your friendship. The blind lady holding the scales of justice represents justice created by the so called justice system.

Like I've said before I'm not a big fan of Vladimir Putin of Russia but I totally agree with him when he said that some people should not be entitled to a trial. He may have everything else wrong but he has that one statement right. It has gotten where everyone is a target for some demented asshole that sets out to murder people for whatever reason. One good way of reducing the crime rate is for everyone to carry a firearm. At present people seem to be open season for every thug in town because they know that the ordinary citizens aren't armed.

When a police officer confronts a subject they simply waste their time and jeopardize themselves by yelling for the subject to drop his gun. If the subject has committed a crime with the firearm and steps out of his car holding the firearm then save your breath and possibly your life and simply shoot the sorry bastard. I'll take it one step further than what Vladimir Putin advocates. If some people shouldn't be entitled to a trial then I personally feel that there are some people that shouldn't be entitled to live. If a person murders someone then that person should forfeit their own life.

Corruption breeds corruption and it involves itself in police departments as much as in all public positions. I've said it before and I'll keep saying it until hell freezes over. Being a lawyer should disqualify anyone from holding public office. A lawyer holding a public office is nothing more then having a fox guarding the hen house. Take it fro me a lawyer doesn't give a rat's ass about right or wrong because all they care about is winning the case anyway they can.

As I grew older the one thing that became apparent to me that I couldn't understand was that all of the husbands 1 came into contact with didn't seem to have any balls because their wives seem to control everything. One cute little neighbor couldn't seem to keep her nose out of everyone's business and another nosey neighbor thinks he's the high sheriff of the entire development. Take some good advice and if you're happy where you're at right now don't move. I moved into a nice restricted neighborhood and found myself surrounded by pricks.

My wife and I own and drive a 1996 Chevrolet truck with 300,000 miles on it. It has been falling apart for the past three years and I was hoping that maybe I could buy us a nicer vehicle before I kicked the bucket but I had some freeloading trailer trash file a lawsuit against me based solely on perjury and I had to pay the trash $125,000.00. If you want to see how the Rule of law can destroy an innocent person's life read the book Kangaroo Justice.

Due to that bunch of thieves led by money grubbing lawyers it looks like the only nice vehicle that I'll get to ride in is in the back of the hearse taking me to the cemetery. Funerals suck as far as I'm concerned who the hell would like to lie in a casket and have people gawking at them and making comments about how they look.

TO HELL AND BACK!

If anyone is curious as to why this book is entitled " Innocent Until Proven Guilty --My Ass! Then read the book Kangaroo Justice and you'll have a good understanding why. If you've ever been screwed up one side and down the other by a lying ass lawyer and a nimble headed judge then the concept of being innocent until proven guilty doesn't mean too much.

The lawyers are milking the weed killer Roundup until they can get every dime out of that lawsuit that they can possibly get. It's agreed that Roundup has caused cancer in people that have used it. Besides Roundup it has also been discovered that Johnson and Johnson baby powder has caused cervical cancer in women. Every since I was a teenager women have sprinkled Johnson and Johnson's baby power on their crotch and panties for hygiene purposes.

Here's a news flash for you. It's a proven medical fact that men can get throat cancer from eating a woman's vagina. It doesn't take a rocket scientist to understand why there's an epidemic of throat cancer among men and what has caused it. I've been a student of oral sex my entire life and have been exposed to Johnson and Johnson's baby powder on most occasions. There's a good chance I'll come down with throat cancer due to me indulging in an accepted past time. It amazes me that men just won't file a lawsuit against Johnson and Johnson. Maybe they just don't want the world to know that they are muff divers. It doesn't make any sense to me because I've always worn my muff diving as a badge of honor. If I ever come down with throat cancer I certainly won't hesitate to file suit against Johnson and Johnson baby powder for giving me throat cancer.

Yes sir, I've been to hell and back pushed there by two lying ass lawyers and a brain dead circuit court judge in Asheville, North Carolina. All of them were quite happy to lie about everything in order to steal every dime I had to live on. Hopefully all the sorry bastards will die a painful death and rot in hell where they belong. After twenty five years in law enforcement I can honestly say that the biggest assholes that I ever come across were lawyers and judges. Even now they do everything that they can do to destroy America. It appears that any city that is controlled by the Democrats and other liberals permit racist mobs to burn, loot and destroy everything they want to. The morons burn all the businesses in their part of town, destroy statues of our history. Any city controlled by the Democrats are controlled by Democrats that just sit on their ass and do nothing. The blacks are basically racist that enjoy breaking into the businesses and stealing everything they can carry out. The sorry little assholes set up areas in the city and don't want the police coming into the areas. As far as I'm concerned all of the rioters are nothing but common trash and should be met with enough force to stomp hell out of each one of them. The sooner the worthless trash is eliminated the better off America will be. For myself I'm sick and tired of seeing mobs of freeloaders marching around carrying their dumb ass signs and assaulting police officers. Talk about being stupid the assholes burn everything in their neighborhoods. If they really want a good fight then come into the residential neighborhoods of white people and start burning their homes and property.

It's high time for freedom and liberty loving people to put an end to the brainless trash wrecking our country and destroying our heritage and culture. I guarantee you that almost everyone of the trash are free loading pimps that are milking the system of every dollar that they can get out of it. No doubt they're the same ones that attend colleges and raise hell with every conservative that comes to the college to speak. Most of the college professors are assholes that are hell bent of making America a socialist country.

As I said in one of my books either love America or get your sorry ass out of the country. If anyone writes a book and expresses their point of view you can rest assured it won't be sold or distributed by anyone. No one cares about your point of view unless you happen to be a host on Fox News. Anyone on Fox News can write a book about how to pick up a turd from the clean end and within a week it will be New York Times best seller.

Don't waste your time and money.